How to save Lucy

Loren Joslin

Copyright © 2022 by Loren Joslin

All rights reserved.

No portion of this book may be reproduced in any form without written permission from the publisher or author, except as permitted by U.S. copyright law.

Contents

This is me..

"Lila, we got to go baby." I whispered to my little girl, in hopes to not let her dad hear us while he slept on the couch. I peered at him to make sure I didn't wake him. Nope, breathing still slow and steady mouth slightly ajar. Empty beer cans sitting on the stand beside him.

I quickly slipped Lilas jacket on her little arms but not without wincing at the tugging motion. Shit... today is not going to be easy. I hope it's a light day for us. Lila and I slipped out the door without Emmett hearing us.

After dropping Lila off at the daycare down the street in I got in my orange Datsun and drove to the precinct. Going in I rushed off past the others bag in tow slipping into one of the stalls to dress in peace so Lopez or Harper didn't see the aftermath of Emmett's drunken nights. He has a stressful job, he's a firefighter and yesterday the lost someone on a call... I know how hard handling on the job deaths can be, I am a cop after all. But, with Lila around I could never imagine fighting back to stop him... I can't let her see me like that.

"Hey mama, how's Lila today?" Lopez asked while we tied hair up in low buns. "Adorable as alway." I smiled think of my light. My almost 2 year daughter who keeps me going and going strong. "She just had to wear her purple tutu to daycare today with her princess crown." I smiled thinking of her smiling at me as she did a little twirl, making my way to roll call.

Walking in with on a minute to spare she immediately felt the scrutinizing eyes of Tim... judging her for almost being late, almost willing her to do better. Thinking about it she bumped into a chair, inhaling sharply at the moment of pain she felt. Looking to make sure no one noticed quickly she noticed everyone having conversations. That ended abruptly at the sound of the door closing.

"Chen? Are you waiting for permission to sit? Or are you going to stand there like your special?" That earned a few chuckles. Lucy took a deep breath and said, "sorry sir." Quickly taking a seat as 2 detectives come in the room. We go through roll and then disperse. Outside of the room I run into Nolan who informs me that Tims wife was shot and left for dead in a dumpster last night AND that his home was broken into by the guy he shots brother. "They have me on desk duty again til IA straightens this whole mess out." IA is ran by my best friend/fellow Rookies dad Jackson's dad. He's a reasonable man by tomorrow Nolan will be back on the streets.

I saw Tim in the hallway speaking to one of the secrecies on Isables case and go up to him, "Hey, I'm so sorry about Isabel." "Yeah, thanks. Go kit up our shop, ask Mike for the Bradford special."   I give him my best confused face and ask, "what's that?" He gives me a short, "you'll see" and stalks of.

After kitting up I start my pre vehicle inspection. Tim walks out and tells me to shut the trunk. I pause momentarily thinking of how to do it without giving myself some added pain due to the strain. I take a deep breath and squint my eyes hoping he's distracted. And grab the trunk slammming it shut. I can feel his eyes browsing into my skull as I fight back the tears.

"What's the matter, boot?" He comes up to me touching my elbow suddenly causing me to flinch.

"Ah, nothing just got a little carried away at the gym sparring." I quickly dismiss it getting in the shop quickly.

Tim quickly drives to the Bronson Estates. Word has it we got a lead the person responsible for leaving Isabel for dead, Vance, is in there. "Let's gear up! You got your back up piece?" Tim asks. I nod at him curtly as he hands me silver metal piece. "What's this?" I raise an eyebrow at him. "Trauma plate for your vest, little extra protection." I look at him with knowing eyes, "oh Bradford special, you really think we're going to need this?" He helps me place as he informs that they call it Bronson Estates because a movie called Death Wish started a Charles

Branson and that going to calls here used to mean you had a Death Wish... I gulped and looked at him. I always worried about getting shot on the job leaving Lila, to fend for herself against Emmetts drunken rages... so far he has spared her but without me there, who knows what he would do. LAs finest, my ass... if only the LAFD or LAPD that wasn't me knew, who he really was.   I cleared my head and looked at Tim as WeT approached me telling me how crazy things have been and that he never expected all this Drama between Nolan and Isabel his Rookie year. I went to reply to him but Tim said, "Let's go." He has a rifle but Lopez says something to him that has him put it away and we enter the building.

"Alright Boot, we are going straight to Cesiah's apartment." Cesiah is Vance's girlfriend. "Now she won't answer to a uniform so stay off to the side she can't see you with the peep hole. Let me do the talking. I nodded my head at him.

Once in we were both taken aback to her very large pregnant belly. Tim played on this to get her to call by promising her an out and getting her to lower Vance to her apartment. After a while he showed up but he knew something was up and didn't immediately come in. After some talking and buying time before someone answers.   I hear , "Lucy." Frim Cesiah. "My water just broke." I remembered when my water broke it was scary. But Emmett was the ever dotting partner holding my hand supporting me . This was before, before his first loss on the job, before he changed.

I snap myself from the thoughts and get Cesiah to lean back. And look to Tim who assured me we would get them first. I talked calmly to Cesiah and waited till it was time, realizing I would deliver her baby and keep them safe, hell or high water. No woman deserves to go through what she is going through.

We don't deserve it.

That's when I heard fire and Tim yells to Vance that he could hurt Cesiah buying us just a little more time.... He wouldn't leave without her , that we knew. If he did it would be because he was in cuffs. I trusted Tim though. Tim would keep us safe... and I would deliver this baby safely... and then keep them safe.

Cesiah was well into labor screaming and breathing heavily. "Just breath, okay I know it sounds cliche but it will help, I promise." I assured her as I held her hand comforting. "Have you done this before?" She asked once the contraction was over. "Yes I have, but I also aced delivering in the academy." Tim looked back at me. I managed to keep my daughter a secret to everyone but Jackson and Lopez... Jackson picked me up from work bumping into Emmett and Lila leaving for daycare. I begged him to stay quite but he let it slip to Lopez but they both have my secret, til now... I let it out . "I promise to protect you and your baby." I looked her deep in her eyes to gain the trust I knew we both needed. "I'll be right back." I went to get a towel and Tim looked at me, "why didn't you ever say anything?"

"It never came up." He held my arm and looked in my eyes for just a few more seconds . God There really blue... the attraction I felt for this man was nothing I have ever felt for Emmet even when the times were good. But he would kill me and Tim's my TO it can't go past this little school girl crush. To break the awkward moment I asked. "This is another test ain't it?"

"They don't stop just cause we're pinned down, and let's face it you'd think less of me if they did." I smiled at him and went back to Cesiah who looked like she ready to have that baby.

As the light kicked back on Cesiah was doing her final push. I caught the baby cleaned them both up and handed Cesiah her baby wrapped in a towel , "it's a girl." "Good job, Boot." Tim looked at me with pride and then back to the make shift peep stick. "Somethings not right."

He was cut off by the sound of crashing, "lookout!" Tim exclaims as vances guy, pony, pulls his weapon on me. As I reach for mine it's too late and he gets a shot on me. Knocking me backwards and out.

I awake to hearing disgruntled struggling and pleading. I feel a pain in my chest ... silently thanking Mike for the Bradford special as I take my trauma plate out inspecting the job it did.

Tim looks relieved as he sees me moving , "get him!" He says. Throwing the guy off I knew the gunman behind the knee taking him down. We both take on respective men, and place them under arrest.

After things calm down Tim insists on me being looked at by a EMT ... I hold my breath that means they will want to look at my chest where I probably am sporting a new bruise.

"Boot, you can either go to the rig willingly or as an order." As he says that Emmett approaches us. "What's going on Luce, Bradford?" He looks between us. "Lucy took a bullet to the chest and I want her looked at before she goes back to patrol. Don't need her going down on me because we missed an injury." "Lucy?" Emmett turns facing me so no one sees his face. He looks pissed. He hates that I run with Tim. He also probably isn't happy I was so wreckless someone could have seen my various healing bruises under my shirt along with my pretty new one from last night. "I'm fine, Tim." "She said she's fine, is that going to be a problem Tim?" Emmett narrows his eyes at Tim trying him. I'm inwardly thankful for his intervention because I can't let anyone know. They would see me as weak, and incapable of doing my job. Or worse they won't believe me and Emmett takes my Lila, my light, from me. After all he's a respected Firefighter with years under his belt, I'm a rookie whose name is not known yet. Who would believe me? Tim didn't back down. He glared right back at Emmet and I had to hand it to him he was pretty intimidating when he stares. Not scary like Emmett but definitely not a puppy. "I'll look her over." Emmet gave in leading me to the rig.

"Are you fucking serious Lucy. Are you trying to get me in trouble?" He whispered yelled at me, grabbing me by arm once inside.   "No I turned it down. I would not have gave in... I swear." I stuttered at him....   "If you give me away I swear to god I will end you Lucy Chen and you will never see your daughter again, you hear me?" He pushed me down roughly pulling my shoulder the wrong way as he did it. He exited went over to Tim said something angrily and stocked off. "Well he cleared you let's go, Boot.

Tim didn't let it go that I had tried to deny car. He said if I'm so good and didnt need attention I could do push up. My arms, my chest and ribs burning at the pain. Emmett hurting my shoulder made it almost impossible. But the thought of losing my daughter pushed me through.

Truthfully if it was t for the bruises I was hiding I would have taken Tim up on the medical care because getting shot hurts like a bitch. Trauma plate or not.

The rest of my shift went pretty eventful, a few traffic stops. Push ups. Tim death stares with his gorgeous blue eyes.

Oh That Smell

The next morning I awoke early getting Lila ready quickly and out the door before Emmetts , return. Thank God the LAFD runs on 24 hours... but tonight, oh tonight well. Be hell...

My shift went by pretty uneventful. I rode with Captain Andersen per her request. I managed to make a fool of myself... let my suicide talk down, jump... ducked to avoid a pinch BUT managed to let Captain Andersen take the blow...

But other than that, pretty boring. My body was thankful for the break of beating... til tonight.

After subduing a suspect for disloading a firearm "Hey.." he said "I'm not talking to you." I'm still mad at him for all push ups and the commanding me shit... it's not like it was a call. It was my health. "I was an ass" I breath a little in and gag... "Oh god and you smell like it too, what happened?" "Skunk. Apartment. Now enough with the questions boot." Instead of going home I went to get Lila from daycare and then went to the corner. I grabbed all stuff I needed to remove skunk chemicals from Tim's skin stopped at the pizza place and got a large pizza.

"Home?" Lila asked pointing outside. "No baby we are going to mommy's friends. But shhh we can't tell daddy." "Okay mommy."

We pulled up to Tim's and I got Lila out of the car. Grabbed the bag and pizza and we walked up to the door.

"Hello," Tim said then stopped and looked between us. "Boot, little Boot.." he nodded at us both. I smiled. "I come bearing gifts." He opened the door and motioned us in. "Where's your kitchen, because you smell like tomato's and ass... i have a mixture to wash all those oils away and leaving you smelling like normal." "Thanks. Though those double doors to the left." He pointed. I took lilas hand and the stuff and we went in. "What's her name?" He asked me swallowing roughly. "Lila." I said. "Hi Lila, I'm mommy's friend Tim. I keep her safe at work and she keeps me safe. Do you like cartoons?" "Paw patrol." She said. He turned the little Tv on and I got to work on the paste. Tim and Lila talked about the paw patrols and he dug out some paper and high lighters.

"Here go wash up." I'll clean up this mess. I handed Tim the concoction and he walked away. I heard my phone going off but ignored it knowing it was Emmett.... Man was I in for it.

"I'm going to need that recipe boot, it worked like magic." "Family secret," I smiled and tapped my temple. "Beer?" He asked looking between me and Lila. I nodded at him. He grabbed plates and passed them out. We sat down and ate. "So how did riding with Anderson go?" "It was good. I felt like I made an ass out of my self. But I learned a lot. Did you know she's ex marines?" "No shit?" "Swear. We had a jumper today... I didn't talk him down... and I looked." He stopped. Swallowed his beer and said, "It wasn't your fault." He grabbed my hand and looked at me deeply. "I know that, now..." I nodded. We bullshitted about work and I heard my phone ring again... "I really should get her home." I nodded to Lila. "Thanks for the beer." He walked us out and thanked me for everything.

When I got home Emmett was immediately at the door, I could smell alcohol on his breath. "Where the fuck where you?" "Working." "No you weren't I went to get Lila from daycare and they said you picked her up out of uniform ." He said pushing me into the house causing me to trip. "Where did you have my daughter?" Lila squealed being scared. "Let me put her to bed and we can talk." I said pushing past him. And I knew he let me. I picked Lila up took her in the room, changed her into a night time pull up and pajamas. I turned on a movie for her and kissed her goodnight. Knowing If I didn't hurry up , Emmett would be in here. I walked out and immediately was met with his hand across my face.... This never happens. He always go for somewhere that can't be seen. The tears streamed down my face. "Where were you Lucy? Where out being a whore with that TO of yours? I swear to god I will ruin your career."

"He was sprayed by a skunk on a call, I made him a paste at the station then took it to him and left."   He connected his fist with my eye... "your not going to work tomorrow... I'll call you off in the morning. Your sick." He pushed me aside and went to his couch drinking another beer. I climbed into bed and cried myself to sleep.

The next day he left work . Me and Lila made breakfast and watched movies. When I showered I avoided looking into the mirror. "Mommy booboo." She pointed at my eye. "Yes baby. Mommy got hurt at work." "No daddy." She said. I let the tears flow again.

Sometime after lunch we both fell asleep watching a movie...

The sound of pounding woke me up. "Boot I know your home, I see your piece of shit car here." Pound pound pound. I panicked looking in the mirror. What do I say? "Open up now that's an order." I opened the door...   "Lucy..." I immediately saw the hurt and anger in his eyes. "Is he here? I'll kill him." "No . And it wasn't Emmett. I was attacked in the driveway." I lied . "I brought you lunch. He pushed his way around and look around.." his eyes stopped on Lila. "You have a great kid." He said with a small smile. "She is pretty great." I smiled at her as well. Tim reached for my face causing me to flinch. He grabbed me by my chin gently. His eyes inspected my face and he looked serious. I loved his touch, so much more gentle than I'm used too.

Dammit Lucy, what kind of a cop are you? Getting beat my your boyfriend, falling for your TO, if other people knew I'd become a joke; a laughing stock.

"If I found out your lying to me, I'll make you jog behind the shop for a week." "Understood sir." I said. "Thanks for lunch. See you tomorrow." I smiled softly as I shut the door behind him.

Plain Clothes Day

The last couple days have past by uneventful... Emmett tried to play nice apologized and even called work to call me off using his LAFD pull to keep me out of trouble even as a Rookie. My face mostly healed now is easy to hide with make up. So I am back to work in time for my 100th shift as a Rookie, well what would be if it wasn't for Emmett ...

"For your first 100 shifts your training officers have been there to guide the way but not today."   Anderson said to me Nolan and Jackson.

"Plain clothes day." Jackson stated with a nod. "That's right officer west, very good." She praised. I rolled my eyes, he comes from a legend family, his dad being IA and all raised by a LAPD cop. But I was still confused, "I'm sorry what is plain clothes day?" "Your TOs will be out of uniform riding with you in a strictly observational capacity." Grey said and Anderson added to it with a little more detail .

And of course Nolan made a crack about choosing where to get lunch . I stifled a giggle once she said that we should be scared. "What happens if we get into real trouble?" I asked now feeling the scared. "Deal with it and if you can't your TO will step in." Grey said. "Make no mistake if that happens you will be judged. That's it. Good luck out there." Anderson dismissed us.

Nolan went on about us finally getting to call the shot and Jackson threw out a statistic that 20% of rookies wash out from plain clothes day.

I got my kit and headed to the shop. Tim was leaning against the wall looking as good as ever in his plain clothes. "What are you doing?" I asked him. "Filled our your evaluation." He held it up between his fingers. "But we haven't even left yet." I pointed out. "Yeah. I already know how today's going to go." I scoffed and got in the rig. I soon realized that I was in the passenger got back out looked Bradford in the face "no you don't. You're just trying to get in my head but it won't work." I then stalked to the driver seat and got in.

"Don't open it til end of shift." He handed it to me and I informed him he would be proven wrong.

I tried making small talk and he reminded he wasn't here. So I kept driving then I spotted someone with a video camera at the electric box. I thought out loud about how weird it was... then I noticed he was filming a woman in her bedroom... oh god just gross and so so wrong. The poor woman. Knocking him over with the door I cuffed him and called it in. "Did you include this in your evaluation officer Bradford?" I smirked. He just kept his hard face and got back in the shop.

After calling it in I found out my suspect was a tier 3 sex offender. And I had to flaunt it to Tim.

I went over my checklist out loud. "What?" I ask him. "Didn't say anything." "But you're giving me the look." "What look?" "That look. What, am I missing something? No don't answer that." "Wasn't going to." "Good because I made a solid pinch here. All right let's go."

Back at the precinct After getting my suspect booked I pulled out the envelope. I couldn't resist . I opened it to find another envelope that said "I said AFTER your shift" " I know everything your going to do Boot. Just like when you didn't process all your suspects property." I then listed everything off to him that I did and he asked me how the suspect got there.

"He drove like I said I have his car keys"

He pointed out that most child sex offenders have sick videos and photos to lead to bigger busts in their cars and I didn't have his car. SHIT.

Arrests like this make me worry for my Lila growing up in the gross gross world. What if this guy was near my daughter and I didn't even know it? What if someone at her daycare was a sex offender who wasn't caught yet... I made a mental note to run all the names of all the employees and there accomplices...

I discovered that his phone had a text saying to get his van! And there was a blue work van right there!

I raced back to the arrest site no vehicles. Dammit! I called in a reverse directory on the van and dispatch informed me it was impounded. I looked at Tim. "What? You had the van impounded?" "Once it was clear you overlooked the detail." He nodded at me. I scowled at him. "But then why did we race over here?" "So you could discover your own mistake that's what today's all about Boot." He reached towards me to turn the hazards on and I flinched, he didn't miss it. "You know I also don't like being lied to boot. I will figure out what really happened to you. And when I don't I won't take it easy on you." I frowned and ignored him. "And what you get bonus points to humiliate me?"

He went on about me getting rattled by a look. Little did he know just his presences gets me rattled. "Your talking an awful lot for a silent observer." I pointed out as I pulled away to patrol again.

We went and got lunch at the place that has my favorite veggie burger and pickle chips but that was cut short by a call about a noise disturbance. We arrived on scene and I immediately knew the disturbance. A endlessly barking dog who was just so adorable... I hope it has food and water out here in this heat. "Hello? LAPD anyone home? Hey girl it's okay." I told the dog.

"Not exactly what I meant by control the environment." Bradford told me. I rolled my eyes at him. And looked at the neighbor trimming her hedges. "That dog barks all the time." "Ma'am do you know if the dogs owner is home?" I looked around for sign of life as she mmhmm'd at me. No sooner did a person coming walking out kicking dirt at the poor door dog. "Shut up! Shut up Missy!" "Hey woah there's no need for that." I said. "Honey there's no need for that I can treat my dog however I want." He snapped. Mr Acker and Emma had a few words about the dog and the fact that she called. He kicked dirt at the dog again after a rough "shut the hell up." I informed him that if I even got a wiff that he was abusing the dog I will make him my personal project. "How's that for controlling the environment?" I asked Tim as we got in the shop. "Listen that was a little rough he doesn't like the type to let the way you talked to him slide, Luc... I mean boot." "Im sorry, I just felt so bad for that dog. Did you see her?" I smiled "Mmhmm..." I caught him glancing at me... god I wanted to reach out and touch his hand... oh god Lucy Chen get it together he's your TO I have Emmett... Sure enough we got called back to Sargent Greys office who informed me that Acker did file a complaint and that I'm meeting with her tonight. Tim made a comment about me washing out and I scoffed at him. "Another thing, the daycare called here and said that Lila was picked up by her dad." I froze. Emmett never picks isla up without me knowing. I checked my phone. No message.   "I didn't know you had a daughter."   "Yeah I try to keep that under wraps. But that is seeming more and more difficult. Thank you sir."

"Tim. I have to go check on her." "I'm just here in plain clothes Lucy. It's up to you what we do." I got in the shop and called dispatch to put us on a personal, unless a complaint about little Missy comes through again. To let me know. God this could cost me my career. But I'm worried about her. I don't trust Emmett , he has been to nice lately. "Lucy? You okay? Your knuckles are white." "Yes, I just need to make sure Emmett knows about her medicine." I lied again... god I hate lying to Tim.

"Your lucky I have a soft spot for kids Boot , or I'd be adding this to my report."   "Thank you sir." I nodded at him as we pulled up to my house.

"Uh Emmett?" "MOMMY!" Lila came running for me jumping in my arms. "Lila baby, is daddy being good to you? Having fun?" I looked around no Emmett. "He's packing our clothes mommy, says we're going to Nunna's! Yay Nunna!" I stiffened.

I rushed with her in my arms to Islas room. Sure enough her bedazzled Star Wars suitcase was open. "Where do you think your taking her?" "My moms. Your not stable enough to watch her when I'm on shift." "Like hell I'm not." I told him. "I'm off at 5:30. That leaves plenty." "I said what I said Lucy. Lying saying you were attacked... what's wrong with you? Being a rookie is getting to your head." He shoved me... "MOMMY!" Isla screamed. "Shut her up." I grabbed her and whispered comforting words in her hair. "Your not taking her Emmett. She can come with me the rest of the day I won't take dangerous calls and Tim's in plain clothes." "The hell you will..." "Boot! We gotta go... Theres trouble at Ackers again." "Officer Bradford, I have to bring Lila with us, Emmett got called into work early..." I said. "Let's go Boot, get a move on." I grabbed Lila without a second thought of the consequences later. Tim put the car seat in that was on the porch for the sitter when Emmett and I worked weekends and we was off. He turned the dash cam off. "Whats this about?" He asked as we drove Ackers. "Oh Emmett was going to surprise her with a day at the park but got called into work early so he was going to take her to his moms but she called and said she wasn't feeling well..." he looked at my knowing eyes. I breathed out slowly... this such a mess.

"I'm saving your job. Stay here.." he said. Tim left me in the car. Once he spoke to Acker we were about to leave and I noticed Missy scratching at the garage door and a nasty stain. I grabbed a scope. "Uh hold on, is that blood? Could be blood." Tim told me if I was wrong I could get in more trouble and all Acker would get is more money.

I didn't care I opened my door, walked back to the garage. Acker protested me opening it, I did anyway and found a dead Emma. "It was an accident she she got in my face. She just wouldn't shut up!" He tried to resist me but I succeeded putting him under arrest. I called in for another unit to transport him so I wouldn't put in harm. I told Missy she was a good girl.

Thankfully Lopez and Jackson came. I informed Jackson with what I told Tim and he we was more than happy to transport the suspect. Since it's up to him today. I could get used to this. Too bad for now it's only one day.

Since it was almost end of shift I took Lila into the precinct with me and Bradford followed. "End of shift Boot. Don't you want to read your evaluation?" "Why captain is probably going to fire so what's it matter now?" I asked showing Isla where to color. "Just do it." He touched my hand and we locked eyes for a second. "Officer Chen second guessed every decision she made. " "The whole point of doing this was to get under your skin." He smiled at me with a crooked smile. "Clearly you did sir." I nodded. "Besides for helping me out and I appreciate it." I told him softly. "Yeah, until the end. Because when it really counted, you didn't hesitate. You put it all on the line, and you made the right call. Which really pisses me off because now I got to rewrite the damn thing." He ignored my second comment but he smiled and nodded so I knew he understood. He tore the paper up.

"Tim what's going to happen to me?"

"Officer Chen, step inside." Anderson told me. "Go ahead I got her." He nodded at Lila.

Tim's POV Once Lucy was inside I kneeled down beside her beautiful daughter whose skin was only slightly darker than Lucy's and she had long for her age pretty black hair. Super curly.   "Hey Little Boot, what happened with daddy?" "He pushed mommy then you came in." She continued coloring without looking at me. "Does he do that often?" She nodded. SON OF A BITCH. I'll kill him. I'll set a fire and trap him inside in the call. I'll kill him. I huffed.   And Lucy. Oh sweet Lucy. She can't know I know. Not yet... but I will save her. How I wish I didn't get assigned the hotshot 100 shifts ago. Then she could be mine...

"Bradford your turn!" Anderson stated.   Lucy came out and smiled letting me know she was safe.

After my meeting and giving Anderson my evaluation and a little ear beating about telling Lucy not to threaten civilians again I went and changed. Her and Lila were gone. I went to the parking lot finding Chen helping her in the car.   "Hey? Want to grab dinner? We need to talk." I told her.   She nodded and I told her we're to meet me. I followed her to the diner.

Once in there we sat down.   "Now Chen, you can't do that again. What happened today... Lila could have seen something she shouldn't have. Or been hurt." "I know, I know. It's just I was stuck Tim. It won't happen again."   "Eat up. Boot." We talked about our meetings with Captain and ate in almost silence besides Lilas cute little comments and talking about the sirens she heard on the way to Ackers. And the cute puppy she got to pet. I used the restroom and came back and Lucy had Lila on her hip. "Here's my evaluation of you." She handed me a small envelope. "That's not how it works Boot." "Yeah well if you don't want to open it, don't." She smiled turned and walked away. I opened it and it was the bill. "That little ..." I smiled shaking my head ... oh Lucy Chen you will be the death of me.

Confessions

After getting Lila in the car and driving home I see Emmett is gone. I let out a breath I was holding and got Lila out and headed in the house.

We decided to go in the backyard and she played with her toys while I thought of how to escape this mess. I know Emmett won't let today go. I can't run to my parents. They haven't spoke to me since I told them I was pregnant. All my Officer friends would just ask questions. And I have no clue what to do with Lila while I work. The daycare isn't safe . "Mommy no cry?" She said hugged me. And I held on to her for dear life. "I'll save us baby. I will." I told her. We got dressed for bed around 8 and both laid in her bed til sleep took over.

I woke to the sound of the front door closing. I don't keep an off duty piece because of the fear of Emmett using it against me.... I crept out bed kissed Lila and looked out her door. It was Emmett. "You think your going to pull that shit and get away with it bitch?" He smacked me to the floor. "You can't just take her from me Emmett she's my kid too. Who does everything for her? Me! You sweep in and be mister fun and laughs I'll give you that. But I do daycare drop off and pick up. Babysitter payment. Feed her bath her." "Your emotional and weak... what happens when you get killed on the job and she has no mom?" "That's what this about? My job. Like yours is any better." "A girl can live without a dad but not a mom? Please you really think being a cop is what's best for us. Or that you in uniform is attractive? Whatever you have going on with Bradford is a joke." I froze. How did he know I liked him? "Yeah Lucy I see it. Why do you think since you joined the academy I changed then when you became a rookie and got paired with that pretty boy I've been being different to you?" "Fuck you. Me and Lila, we are gone tonight." I said and walked away. But not before getting hit in the back of the head and seeing black.

The next morning I woke up with a headache and didn't remember why. I looked around and all the memories flashed back. I looked and looked around and couldn't find Lila or Emmett. Fuck. Fuck. Fuck. That bastard! "Told you not to play with me Lucy. She will be at my moms. You can VISIT whenever." The tears came down. He's did it. He's finally broke me... took my hope my reason for fighting . Knocking on the door. "Let's go Boot, we all got called in. Vice Presidents coming to town. It's all hands on deck." He stopped mid sentence and looked at me. "What's going on..." "Nothing.

Let's go." I was already in sweats and a tank top so I just went and rode with Tim. "Lucy, I know somethings wrong." He barely calls me Lucy. "Where's little boot?" "With her nunna." I said. We were soon at the precinct. I took of to the locker rooms and got dressed. After having a meeting about today's assignments us Rookies stood in line to get our kits. I just thought about Lila. 1 morning without her and I'm already losing it. I felt my eyes tear up. Im going to get an apartment and I'm going to get Lila back and leave Emmett. "I don't get all the fuss it sounds like we're all getting paid over time to just close some streets and hang some signs."

"That's like saying being drawn and quartered is fun time with horses." Tim deduced. "We're literally creating traffic jams during rush hour on purpose."

"Everything we do today is gonna piss someone off." Lopez added her input and turned to the quartermaster. "Quadrant One." And I followed up with mine and Tim's quadrant. "I mean, we deal with angry people every shift, but a day of OT means I can finally get a ... a air conditioner." I wanted to say apartment. Tim chuckled and said something about AC making us soft.

"Are you serious?" Jackson asked.

"As a heart attack, Boot. Which I gotta say you almost gave the watch commander back there." Bradford told me.

"Seriously, playing with your phone during a briefing is a cardinal sin." Lopez looked at me.

"I only hope you were canceling something important, because Grey won't forget that for a while." Lopez smiled at me.

"I had to check on Lila, she went to her nunnas last night and wasn't too happy about it." I felt Bradfords eyes snap up at me and he looked over me with cop eyes trying to read my expression.   We were handed ALOT of gear.   "Is that all for us?" I looked at him and he nodded.

"Yep. Extra road flares for the uptick in accidents. Extra ticket books for the increase in idiots" Tim told me in true Bradford fashion.

Lopez continued "Extra crime-scene tape for blocking sidewalks. And cones for closing roads."   "Okay okay I get it." I groaned. Bradford and Lopez smiled at us and continued. "Oh, we're not done yet. Hats and bats. Tactical helmets and 42-inch batons for riot control, along with heavy-duty vests if things get ugly." "And my personal favorite, the 40-millimeter tear-gas launcher for when democracy gets real." Lopez smiled evilly. "But hey atleast you'll be able to ride in comfort." Bradford told me.

In the shop "So air conditioning? " he raised an eyebrow at me. "You can't lie to me Lucy." "No judgement?" "No judgement." "I'm leaving Emmett." I stated. He smiled widely. "I'm glad my relationship ending makes you happy, sir." I pouted as we pulled up to the homeless camp and stalked out.   Tim announced over the loud speaker "All right, listen up. Until tomorrow at 3:00 p.m., the stretch of Vine between

Melrose and Franklin will be off limits. Sanitation services will be arriving in 20 minutes. You'll have until then to pack up. " He got out then turned to me, "Rope off the block. Make sure everyone moves off." I woke up a guy on a bench sleeping and then a fight broke out over sneakers... I intervened getting pulled to the ground but got the upper hand and cuffed and lifted the perp. "Hands behind your back. Don't move. All right stand up." Bradford stopped and stared at me with concern. "Chen." "What." I snapped at him still mad. "Stop dont move." I followed his gaze to my midsection seeing a dirty hypothermic needle sticking out of my uniform. "Chen. Chen." I looked at him and shaked my head. "I I didn't see it, it was on the ground and..." I felt clammy and nauseous and my head hurt like hell. "It's okay but I need to pull the needle out." He told me softly . He then pulls it out carefully and sees the blood on the tip. "What's the procedure when an officer is exposed on duty?" Leave it to Tim to give me a Tim test at a time like this. Answered that I would collect the evidence and go to the nearest hospital that being, Shaw memorial.

He then turns to another cop and tells them something and tells me it's time to go.

"Lucy, I didn't mean to offend you earlier, it's just Lila told me ... that Emmett hurts you." Tim told me on the way to Shaw memorial. "Then I may have watched your body cam footage from the day she ended up with us on duty..." "YOU WHAT!" I screamed at him. "I'm just concerned Lucy...

you've been coming to work hurt and in a daze until we go on a call. I'm sorry." "Tim my life is none of your business." "That's what I told you about Isabel, but who was there for me during it all? Helped me? You, Lucy! You are the reason I came out of that ordeal with my morales in tact." Tim shot at me. And he's right I stopped him from removing heroine from her house, I did allow him to steal narcan for her... but I did it and spared him being the one... i comforted him after she overdosed, after she was arrested and was shot for being a CI. "I know Tim... I'm sorry. It's just I'm struggling...." We then pulled into Shawn memorial. Once inside Tim got me moved ahead of the others to be treated they pulled blood and now we wait.   I pulled out my phone and started scrolling down Google. "Falling down the webmd rabbit hole isn't gonna change your results." Tim came up behind me placing his hand on mine holding the phone. " HIV is three times more prevalent in the homeless community than it is in the general population. Hepatitis is five times more prevalent-" i was rattling off things I was reading. Tim cut me off.. "And cows kill more people a year than sharks. The facts are whatever you make them." "What- What if I get hep C from this needle, and one day I get shot, and you're trying to stop the bleeding and you forget that, you know, you have a you have a cut on your hand? Or worse- a kid gets shot and I'm the one with the cut? Or what if I get cut and I'm with Lila and she gets it and I get her sick..." maybe Emmett is right, maybe I'm a risk to our own daughter and she's better with his mom. "Then you'll be a cop with hep C and a cut. You signed up to put your life on the line. That means your health, too. Lila will be fine, the odds of her ever coming in contact with your blood is so slim. Focusing on fear isn't gonna change the outcome. Lab results are gonna take hours. Do you want to hang out in the worst-case-scenario panic room, or you want to get back to work? Get a apartment, leave Emmett."

"Leave me?" A deep voice booms from the door way. It's Emmetts deep voice. My eyes widen in fear. "Emmett... I – I ... no he doesn't know what he's talking about." I shake my head at him. "I knew you it you whore. Your sleeping with your TO. I'm glad I sent Lila to my moms. A whore for a mother." Tim gets up and stands between us. "You are going to walk out that door right now. This is me doing you a favor. If you don't take it I will arrest you for public disturbance, disturbing the peace and any other thing I can throw at you." "You better watch yourself Lucy, Tim." Emmet throws over his shoulder and storms out. "Go splash some water on your face, let's get back out there." He turns to me. "Okay.." I find the nearest ladies room.

I look in the mirror after using the restroom. "Everything is going to be fine." I tell myself out loud, Lila, the test results, Emmett, my conflicting Tim emotions... when I hear a woman come out of another stall. She tells me about her brother and the accident he had. "I'm sorry is he going to be okay?"

"No." She leaves the room. I look in the mirror and notice a bottle on the floor of the stall the lady had used. I go in and look it's a bottle of bleach with a needle size hole in it. Her brother... she's going to kill him. I race out and follow her to her brothers room. Rachel looks to be injecting him with the needle. "Hey what are you doing!" I asked. "This is what he wants." She tells me, she looks so broken. So scared.   "Stop." I tell her as I draw my taser and Radio Tim to tell him what room I'm in. I then pleaded with Rachel to put it down and that he wouldn't want this.   " Yes, I do. My brother wouldn't want this. He ran triathlons. Being stuck in bed, brain-dead, hooked up to machines forever, that's his idea of hell." "Okay listen to me I know your in pain but this isn't your decision to make." I plead with her again. Man I don't want to taze her... Tim comes in sizes up the situation and then grabs his gun , "Page a trauma surgeon and get an O.R. on standby. Incoming gunshot wound." I heard him say. "Please. Please. Mike never had a chance to sign a DNR. He and my sister-in-law got married six months ago. She's his medical proxy, but she can't let him go. She doesn't see that she's hurting him." "And you think that injecting him with bleach is better? Listen, you have no right to decide if he lives or dies. What you're talking about is murder." "He's already dead"   "Hey, hey. Hey, hey, hey, put the needle down. Put it down. Hey. Look at me. Right here. Right here. Put the needle down, okay?" "No." And she injects the needle and I fire my tazer at her. She drops to the floor.

Tim asked if she pressed. I pull the needle out and tell him she didn't.

"Can't leave you alone for a minute." He shakes his head at me and I just smile sideways at him.

Tim then gets radioed back to the station but tells me to go ahead and wait for my results. "Tim? Thanks." I tell him before he leaves and he pushes. Stray piece of hair out of my face. "For what? Doing my job?" "No for being here. Stoping Emmett from embarrassing me... he's been drinking... never before work. It's not an excuse but it's hard. And you have made it better." "Anytime boot." He moves his hand I didn't realize was lingering on my face.

After he walks away I go sit down. Hands on my chin foot shaking in anxiety. Tears threatening to spill over again. Lila, Emmett, the test, Tim... all in my mind. I can't do this.. it's too much. It's too much.

Tim's POV   On the way back to the station I see Emmetts car driving from the hospital... he turned red on a no turn on red zone I turn on the shop lights and siren pulling him over. I remembered what Lucy said about the drinking. "Good evening Mr. Lang. License, proof of insurance, and registration please. Do you know why I pulled you over?" I asked. "Save it jackass." Emmett bit back. I caught a wiff of alcohol. "Sir have you been drinking?"I asked him. "No." "Well you turned right on a no turn on red, went over the lines and I smell alcohol. I'm going to need you to complete a field sobriety test." "Just breathalyze me. I'm under the legal limit." I nodded grabbed his info. Went back to the shop called in his information and got a breathalyzer. He blew in it with a roll of the eyes and blew 2 points over the legal limit. I placed him under arrest and called a tow truck. Sarg is going to be mad I took so long but this was worth it.

Bada** CopMom

After processing Emmett for a DUI meeting with Grey I headed back to the hospital because West messaged me and told me Lucy was getting her results. I bumped into her as she turned a corner and grabbed her waist to steady her. "Well?" "Just a staph infection. No HIV no Hep C." We both sighed in relief. "I have some news, let's use this room." I pulled her in a empty room. "I arrested Emmett for a DUI and he will also have some tickets for obeying the traffic laws." "You what!" She almost shouted. "That's not all. Your body cam caught footage of Emmett pushing you... I had stagnant Grey pull it. If you have any bruises you can get a temporary PFA on him and it will cover Lila until you guys get things covered." "I uh, I have nowhere to take her yet." West just rented out a 3 bedroom apartment . I peeked in the hallway. "Lopez can I borrow West for a second?" "Sure. Boot you heard the man." She said. "West can Lucy and Lila stay with you?" I asked him. "Sure I've been looking for a roommate." "There you go. LOPEZ." I yelled in the hallway. "Here's officer Chen's house key can you and West go there and retrieve there clothes. Why we take care of something." "Sure but you owe me." Lopez quipped and they walked out.

Lucy's POV "Tim thank you for this.. really." I said to him as he drove me to the station to change and get my car. "I worry about you Boot. You need to be on your game and not hurt and distracted." We pulled in. I went to the desk to file the PFA. "We need proof of abuse Officer Chen." I nodded and looked at Tim who was standing there. "I have body cam footage of him pushing her." Tim said to the officer. "That's not enough... you guys should know that." "Okay, okay, here ." I unbuttoned my shirt. Showed them my arms and rub. I looked at my TO whose eyes were hard and narrow with anger. "Lucy." He whispered. I looked.. you couldn't see a spot of non bruised skin. "Very well. Here's. PFA that includes you and your daughter. It is good for 90 days. Before those 90 days is up you need to get a custody agreement in place and then you can reapply for another long term PFA for yourself only. Unless he proves a harm to your child." The officer said handing me a paper. "I will accompany you in uniform to get Lila back from his parents in case they cause issues." Tim looked at me. "Thank you. I'm going to get changed." I nodded. I got dressed and met Tim outside grabbed the car seat and we rode in the Shop to pick Lila up. When I arrived at Emmett's mother's Time provided the copy of the PFA that issues Lila to come with me.   Emmetts mother is the opposite of Emmett she is kind, caring, and knows that her son is wrong.   "Here you go sweetie. She was an angle. Emmett called me he's in jail for a DUI for 3 days. I hope your using this time to get moved out of his house sweetie." "Thank you Linda."   "Mommy!!! Lila came around the corner and jumped in my arms." "Daddy hurt you. Took me. Now I stay with Nunna." She said. "Oh baby, it's over. We are going far far away from Daddy and he won't hurt me ever again." "I love you mommy." She grabbed my face and kissed me. "I love you sweetie." "Are you ready Officer Chen?" I nodded. He put his hand on my lower back and guided me and Lila to the shop. The ride from Linda's to the precinct is about a half hour. Being that it's late Lila was asleep in minutes. I let the tears flow. "Lucy.... I'm probably speaking way out of TO lane right. But you are an amazing mom, and Officer. You can do both, you realize that right?" He kept his eyes on the road as he spoke "No I can't. Like Emmett told me, I can't do both and I was a fool to think I could be an officer and a mom. I'm a woman a woman in authority is disgusting."

Tim said nothing but pulled over. He gently grabbed my chin, "Lucy Chen, you are far from disgusting, or a bad mom. You are kind and caring. As soon as your off shit your with your daughter. You support her and care for her and that makes you beautiful." He let out a breath and with that I saw his face harden just enough to know he's going into cop mode again,

"So your going to wipe those tears off your face. Your going straighten those shoulders and you are going to be the most badass copmom to little Boot back there. And you are going to show Emmett he is wrong you got that Boot?" I wiped my eyes and nodded. When we got back to the station me and Lila headed to our new home with West.

Reversal

The last few days have been rough... getting Lila used to her new schedule, new daycare and babysitter was not easy. West introduced me to an older lady who watches her while I work at night. Emmett gets out of jail in 2 days. His time got extended due to getting in a fight with another inmate. So his short stay extended a little bit. Which made me sigh in relief. I have since applied for full custody or Lila by use of the PFA and proving that I was the one responsible for most of her car. I have acquired letters of character references from multiple officers, her former daycare, and even Emmetts mom wrote something saying she is better with me.

Today is reversal day. Where cops pose a criminals to rat out dirty cops. This has Tim in a sour mood. As well as the thought of Emmett getting out. Tim does not do well with domestic violence, even on calls.

"I'm just saying, cops don't have the best reputation right now. And if these tests help the public trust us, isn't it worth it?" I argued with him to get him to see the benefits. "And how are we supposed to trust each other if our fellow officers are trying to trick us into screwing up?" He bit back. And man that sounded a lot like what he tried with me and even still does occasionally. "I ask myself that everyday." I bit back. "How's living with West? Little Boot doing okay?" "As best as she can. She excited we got her room set up. I'm getting nervous for him getting out." "Well he can't visit you or come near you. And you live with a cop . You are a cop he would be a fool." Tim told me. "I know it's just he's..." a car horn stops me mid sentence. We see a corvette swerve to pass a car and we turn out lights on to pull the corvette over... I exit the vehicle approach the car as the driver rolls the window down it appears to be Mario Lopez ... I get dazzled by the fact that he's famous but Tim just goes on with job. "License and registration." Mario Lopez tries bribing him with tickets and compliments to me. Mid way through he spots someone across the street and they exchange words about how this was a role reversal and some very not funny joke about Isabel. I felt bad for Tim. His ex wife put him through hell with a drug addiction... I helped him through it just like he's helping me. He then has me write Mario up for everything he can think of. We then return to our shop. "Doesn't all those tickets make you feel better?" "No, I won't be in a better mood til this days over." "How about if you turn the grumpy off I'll treat you and Lila to pizza and a movie." I bribe. "Don't bring Little Boot into this."

Next thing I know we are dispatched to a 459 at 117 Ayers. Tim turns lights and sirens on and hauls ass to the scene while I confirm the call. When we arrive we see Shrooms and a man on the floor with a bear trap on his leg. Tim swears it's another role reversals when he offers us half the drugs in the house. The leg bleeds profusely proving it is a real injury so I call it in to the paramedics. "Tim you need to treat all these calls real. I'm serious now... he could bleed to death!" "WHAT!" "Oh shush you'll be fine I'm making a point." "Tim pizza, beer and a movie with Lila if you take this day serious from now on." I apply regular belt above the mans wound to stop the bleeding. "Fine your right!" Tim snaps and walks away. After the paramedics come and call us idiots for removing the trap they said his leg would be okay. We loaded into the shops and headed back to the station. "You're lucky his leg's gonna be okay." I gave him a pointed look. "If Murphy hadn't gotten in my head, that never would've happened. Blame the reversals, not me." "What happened between you two? Did she investigate you or something?" I asked because it's not like Tim to get this cranky over something so stupid. "Indirectly." He nodded at me "Is it Isabel?" I asked putting a hand on his shoulder. "Look, Murphy was her investigating officer." He looked me in the eyes and I saw so many emotions flood through his blue eyes "Okay, but you're not Isabel, so what's her beef with you?" "Not your concern. Start the paperwork." Talk about a smack in the face... his eye softened in remorse.

But... He walked away... I ran into Anderson and we had a conversation about the role reversals and I was on my way back out to the streets where Tim barely said 3 words to me unless it was about work.

After shift I stop and got dinner at the food truck with the other rookies, I also got Lila a take out box to take back to her with me and West. I walked Nolan to his truck and as he got in his truck I hear an automatic gunfire. I swing up his door open and got behind it. As soon as the shooting stopped I ran in the direction it took off. Going back to Nolan I told him there no was no sign of the shooter. "Yeah, patrol found the car he escaped in. It was reported stolen this afternoon. SID is all over it." Bradford comes running up, "Lucy are you okay?" He holds me out at arms length and his eyes get big. "You were grazed, boot." He looks at my arm closer. "I'm fine. I didn't even realize it til now. I promise." "Who'd you piss off?" Bishop asks Nolan. "Clearly someone with access to heavy weaponry." Tim says looking at my arm again. "EMT now , or no work in the morning. Can't work with a hurt boot." "I didn't recognize him." Nolan said. "Bring a jump bag over here and look at her will you?" Tim says to an EMT. "According to intelligence, you've been greenlit by Southern Front." "How's a rookie get greenlit before me? I gotta step up my game." Tim said and I smacked him lightly. "It's not a badge of honor." Bishop snapped at Tim. "Violent white supremacist gang wants you dead, you're doing something right." Lopez quipped. "I gotta call the neighbor to get Lila. Be right back. Anyone want chicken and fries?" Tim snatched the bag. "Thank you."   "That arm?"   "Stitches should be needed but she needs to keep it clean and change dressings, and use this to keep it from getting infected." She tossed a tube at Tim. I called the sitter and she was more than happy to spend some time with Lila.   Nolan and Anderson soon left after declaring keeping Nolan safe from this green light is top priority. "Jackson, let's go help guard Nolan tonight. Lilas safe. I don't feel right going home since I was seen with Nolan. You never know." "Like hell, you and Lila can stay in the guest room tonight . Your not going anywhere near Nolan's with him being green lit." "Not your concern." I grabbed Jackson's arm and walked away.   Once at Nolan's I leave Anderson leaving and we tell her our plan and she leaves after telling me to call her directly if needed.   "West and Chen reporting for duty."   "Guys this is sweet but honestly it's unnecessary." "You'd do the same for us". I told him. "So, how do you want to do this? Personally, I'd go with alternating two-hour shifts with a static position plus a rover. Oh, and I have earpieces and walkies, just so we can keep in constant contact." Come on West!!!   "You got anything sweet?" Mmmm I could go for cookies, or cake ... hmmm maybe ice cream. Man I miss Lila ...

The next morning I look outside and see a certain someone's car out there... I grab the coffee pot and pour some into a

To-Go cup and go outside.   I knock on the window Tim looks up from his phone.   "I think you might need some of this..." "Did you sleep?" "No less than 20 minutes no more than 40 you know my rule."   "Drink this. I'll see you in a hour." "You take this." He handed me a baggie with a tube of cream and some bandaging material. I rolled my eyes at him and headed in Nolan's. I walked and West said , "You know, the whole point of guard duty is that we take turns being up so everyone gets some sleep." "You could have left at anytime." Nolan told him. "Yep. No one would have given you grief." "Ohh we got to get to the station. But I gotta call the sitter and tell Lila good morning."   I FaceTime her sitter. "Morning Lila! Mommy misses you." "I miss you too mommy." "We're you a good girl last night?" "Yes I went to bed , i brushed my teeth and said my prayers." "That's good baby. I should see you tonight." I told her and blew a kiss. "I love you to the moon and back baby." "I wuv you moon and back mommy."

Later that day in the bullpen. After seizing the property of a massage parlor ran by the gang that has greenlit Nolan I see Bradford and no other than Detective Murphy having a heated discussion. So I decided to go over and defuse the situation. "Uh, hey, I need you to come check something for me. I want to make sure I'm doing it by the book. Okay? So, come on." I said Tim.   "Hey you know what? If I were you I would ask for another TO." Murphy told me . "Yeah well your not me ma'am."

In the shop.   "Tim will you please talk to me." I said.   "No there's nothing to talk about . Quit trying to psychoanalyze a situation that doesn't exist." "Tim it does exist , you wouldn't get all hard Tim around Murphy for no reason." "Fine you know what! She's right. I did know about Isabels addiction and I still let her work! I didn't turn her in! And you know what Lucy, I could have let her get killed. Or another officer. I knew she had gone too deep undercover. But I kept quite. And that is just as bad as doing. You happy now?" He snapped at me.   "Yes, thank you, for helping me understand. But Tim, you loved her. I believe you were blinded by your love and that you decided not to acknowledge her actions. Trust me I know what it's like..."

Later that night I was laying in bed and my phone rang. Tim... "Nolan and Anderson were held captive. They tortured Nolan by hurting Anderson... they eventually shot and killed her."   "And Nolan?" I feared for the worst.   "He's okay..." "Tim?" "Yeah." "Thank you for calling me." "Goodnight boot." And the call ended.

The next morning we covered out badges with a black bad. My hands were shaking and I wasn't having luck. Nolan grabs it and puts it on with ease.   "Thanks." I felt eyes shooting daggers at the interaction. It was Tim.   "There'll be time for grief later. We have a job to finish. Midas gave up his son. We know where he's headed. Look, I know what's in your hearts. What you want to do more than anything. I'd be lying if I said I didn't want it, too. Word is you kill a cop, you never see the inside of a cell. But that's that's not what Captain Andersen would want. Killing this loser won't honor her memory. Doing our jobs will. And we owe it to her to do it the right way. Agreed? All right, let's go."

We set up a road block to catch Cole.

"Look, you need to know that no matter what happens next, whether we arrest this guy or we kill him, it won't make things better." Tim told me.

"I know that." I told him.z

"No. You only think you do." He put his hand on my shoulder. "Please don't tell me to "use it" - the grief or the anger - to make myself a better cop. I can't handle that right now. Everything with Emmett, Lila, you, now Anderson. It's just too much."

"I wasn't going to. Okay? Grief is grief. It's It's a hole that can't be filled, but over time, it'll shrink enough so that you won't fall in every time you take a step. But trust me, if there's one thing you can use to make yourself a better cop, it'll be her life, not her death." He told me when Grey announced that they were 1 minute out.   He stopped. Lopez announced she had a clear shot . But Cole surrendered with his hands and Grey let Nolan do the honors of arresting him.

Back at the apartment I pulled Lila into a hug and just held her and cried. When there was a knock on my door. I opened it, "Boot, little Boot. Brought juice boxes and beer. Pizzas on the way." It was Tim.

Falling Apart

The next few days were spent with work, Lila, and study-ing. Emmett has sense gotten out and has video chatted with Lila per his pleading I allowed him but that's it til we go to to court in a few weeks. Nolan has frequented the apartment for light study sessions for our exam coming up to see if go to the next phase of training. Tim and I have still been too toeing around each other. I know we both have feelings I can feel it, even though neither of has commented on it. Lila just adores him...

There is reports of a virus that affects the blood stream and pretty much kills. It is contracted by bodily fluids. And it is thought that the creator is planning a deadly attack on LA. Russo and Morgan , 2 detectives will be briefing us in the briefing room with Grey.

"Okay, so here is what we know. At 10:00 last night, this man, Corey Valance, boarded a bus from Phoenix to L.A. He had a partner with him. We have no identification on that man, but we do know that they're part of a fringe nationalist group which believes that Los Angeles stands for everything that is wrong in America." Russo began.

"The two men arrived here at 5:00 this morning. We believe Corey's partner strangled him in the bus station bathroom right after." Grey told us.

"You thinking Cory got cold feet?" Tim asked.

"It seems likely, yes, especially since they came here with this deadly virus.

"Well, that explains the Silkwood shower we just took." Nolan stated , I looked at him confused.

"That was purely a precaution. There is no evidence that the biological agent they were transporting has been released." Morgan told him.

"But we do have every reason to believe that there is an attack planned in the near future." Russo told us all. And I was scared. Scared for me, Tim, Lila, LA.

"What type of virus are we talking about?" I asked finally able to speak. "A weaponized strain of hemorrhagic fever, basically causes you to start bleeding and never stop. And that's how the virus spreads, through contact with bodily fluids. It has an extremely short incubation period and a gruesome pathology. If not treated quickly, it has a 90% fatality rate." I really wished I hadn't asked.

"And if it's treated quickly?" Nolan asked.

"We believe that drops down to around 60%. But the bad news is -" Morgan started but was cut off by Nolan again. "That's not the bad news?" "No. The bad news is, there's only an experimental vaccine. We're flying it here from Atlanta. But there's only a few hundred doses. Nowhere near enough to combat an outbreak."

"So, obviously, the rookie exam will be postponed. The Feds are asking us to be their boots on the ground while they set up a command center here. First order of business to I.D. Corey's partner/killer. So you'll conduct field interviews with the other passengers on the bus." Grey told us.

"Do we think Corey's killer is operating alone now?" Someone asked

"No. We think there's one more, a local who picked him up at the bus station."

"So, okay, this is extremely sensitive. We can't risk the news getting out and causing a panic. That being said, you can warn your immediate families to stay away from populated areas, but no details. Understood? All right. Let's go get these guys."

I grabbed my phone called the babysitter and asked her to get Lila and take her back to my apartment and to have no guests. I told her she was not in danger if she went straight there and straight back. I couldn't tell them more.

We were sent to speak to someone who called in about a bag on the bus they had.

We knocked on the door and Tim identified us as the police. "Took you long enough bags in here." The man said. "Sir we're here about the bus you took from Phoenix." "No kidding I called you guys about the bag." Langston said. "And what bag is that?" Tim asked . "I thought it was mine on the bus. I picked it up by accident. Noticed as soon as I got home. Called right away. Still took you guys like six hours to get here." He told us. I looked at Tim confused. "Uh, sir we're not here about a bag." Tim told him. He looked a little upset. "So you don't have mine?" Tim shook his head and told him no. "Damn it. My computer's in there. I went through this one looking for an address and all I found was some weird science equipment." Me and Tim shared a look... this is not good. "Control this 7–Adam–19 patch me into control please." "Sir did you touch anything here?" Tim asked him. "Is everything okay out there?" I asked. "Yeah just stay in there." I saw him grab Langston and pulled him into a room and shut the door. "Tim no!" A few minutes later Tim asked me if everything was okay. "Uh yeah. The CDCs on their way. Hey you need to come out of there." I started panicking. Tim has became such a safe constant in my life. I couldn't Imagine coming back from losing him. "That's not gonna happen gotta keep this contained Luce" "Tim "It's gonna be alright Boot. You keep your head in the game, okay? Everything's gonna be fine." I felt tears in my eyes. Soon Dr Morgan and her team enter the home, "Officer Chen do you want to tell me what happened here?" She asked. "Yeah, uh, the bus passenger mistakenly grabbed the wrong bag, and the virus must have been in it because he coughed up blood on Tim." I told her as people dressed in hazmat start sealing off interior doors and windows Dr. Morgan got an update on Langston and Tim's conditions. I noticed she didn't mention the vaccine. "Uh where is the vaccine." "Still in the air it should be here in about an hour or so." She informed me. "You can't just make Tim wait in there he might not be affected." She explained to me that it's quarantine rules and then asked Tim if he could look in the briefcase. He had the brilliant idea to use his body cam to let Dr Morgan see everything. He told me to view it and I asked him to please be careful. It's taking everything I have to hold in how scared I am. But I can't risk them knowing my feelings for him and losing him as my TO.

While we are looking I notice in the cam in the background Langston had picked up a chair and is charging Tim with it. Oh no. "Tim! Tim, look out! Tim. Tim!" Langston cracked him with the chair saying that he has to get out of there. Tim uses his tazer to bring Langston down and cuffs him to the bed. I don't hear anything from Tim and I start to breath heavy., "Tim! Tim, are you okay, please talk to me." "It's okay I'm okay, we'll that was fun." He said "We need to get that vaccine here right now." I told Dr. Morgan.

I slide down the door to the room and in my soul I can feel him slide down the other side.

"Hey, I, uh I just checked with Dr. Morgan. The vaccine's minutes away." I told him, lying. "You know, you're good at a lot of things. Lying isn't one of them." He laughed a little. "You think I'm good at things? Can I get that in writing? (a beat) How are you doing? Are there any symptoms yet?" I asked even though I didn't want to know the answer... "I'm sweating like a pig. But it's probably because it's 100 degrees in this room." "It's gonna be okay. I really believe that." I reassured him. I could feel something down deep that told me it was going to be okay. "I'm sure you do. But if it isn't -" I cut him off. "Don't think like that. It's -" "If it isn't, I'm not going out the way my man Pete here just did." "What are you saying?" I knew what he meant but I wanted to hear him say it. "When the time comes I'm going out on my own terms." "Tim I have to tell you something incase things do get bad.." I looked to make sure we were alone. "I think I'm falling for you. I'm so scared for you right now Tim. You have become so much than a TO for me and I need you to fight this. I know because your my TO things can't happen but you need to know." I laid my heart out. "Lucy I feel it too. But I keep shoving it down for the same reason. I promise to fight this so when the time is right we can be together." I wiped the tears coming down my face. "You know Emmett saw it before I did?" I said to him. Taking a deep breath. "Saw what?" "My feelings for you. He said something about whatever I have going on with you was a joke..." "I had no clue what he meant

... till I realized it." "It's not a joke... it's real Lucy I feel it too... and little boot she's just the greatest kid. She's what sealed the deal..." he giggled. I smiled then Dr Morgan walked in and explained that she had the vaccine. She and Tim talked he told her he felt fine and wasn't showing symptoms, "Good. You're right at the edge of what we think is the incubation window. So the fact that you're not showing any symptoms doesn't suck. But we're gonna give you this vaccine just to make sure." She explained to him. She then injects him in the arm. "It's experimental right?" "That's correct. So we're just gonna have to wait and see what happens. Maybe nothing. Maybe you grow horns. But for now, I'd say you might've dodged a bullet." I have a bad feeling about this.

We then go out of the house to the decontamination tent and outside of that my fellow rookies and their TOs are waiting "Hey. I heard you guys saved the day." I told West. "It was a group effort." He said "Glad you're okay." He told me. "Me too. I-I mean that you're okay, too." I told him. My head is still spinning from my conversation with Tim. "How's Tim?" Lopez, his best friend asked "I think he's gonna be all right." I nod when I tell her this because something, something just feels wrong. "That's good news." She said "What now?" Jackson asked. "24-hour observation at the CDC" Then Tim comes out of the tent escorted by two hazmat team workers ... we lock eyes and he smiles a small smile at me. BRADFORD emerges from the tent, escorted by two people in hazmat suits, and head for their vehicle. "I'll bet my pension he just told doctors "Tim Bradford does not ride in a wheelchair." Lopez breaks us out of our trans. "Only way I'm leavin' out of here is on my own two feet." Bishop mocks Tim's voice causing me to smile. "Don't you guys have paperwork to finish?" Tim said in true Tim fashion. "He's back." Lopez laughed and her and Bishop did some weird hand lock. Laughing with each other. "Yeah, he is. So stubborn." And at that second the whole world slowed down as Tim took a step and just went limp and fell to the ground. I froze and it's like the world stopped spinning besides everyone working to help Tim. I couldn't move. I was frozen in place paralyzed with the fear that I'm losing him before I even got him.

Just Boot

Sirens blaring, I feel the air blowing, I see the red and blue lights, I smell the fresh air.

I pull it together in time to be asked if I wanted to ride with Tim I nodded graciously jumping in with them.

I grab Tim's hand and squeeze it. I feel dampness, I see his chest rising and falling, I hear the sirens and I smell sanitizer like in a hospital... In college I learned to calm anxiety down you need to point something you hear, see, feel and smell. And it works.

We roll to a stop and I hear gunfire. I cautiously climb out of the ambulance to help them and to protect Tim and his care team. He needs a doctor. I come up behind Jackson and let him know I'm right behind him. Nolan lands a shot in the attackers shoulder as she reloads. Nolan than ducks back. I start to come out of my spot to try and get a shot when the ambulance doors burst open revealing Tim in a tight white t-shirt he starts shooting. I freeze and stare in awe so glad he's conscious. I almost lost him. I look to see Nolan cuffing her as he calls for a doctor that soon appears. "Are you okay?" He comes up to me after talkIng to Nolan. I nod. "Yeah, I'm I'm just glad your okay. And that this is all over. I need me some Lila loving."

"How about this, I go get checked out. You go get this paperwork done and go home to Lila. I'll call you as soon as I'm discharged." "Yeah sounds good. We need to talk..." "Yeah we do." He nodded and walked away.

After finishing up the boatload of paperwork I head to the sitters and get Lila. Thanking her endlessly for watching her late again. "So Lila, your birthday party is coming up, what do you want to do?" "Have a party with you, daddy and all our friends." I gave her a small smile. "What kind of party do you want?" "Hmmm.... I want lots of pink and lightsabers!" I giggled. Leave it to Lila to want the best of both worlds.

I feel so bad for her. I know she misses her daddy... court is 1 day before the party so hopefully we can have something in place and he will be able to come. I just don't know where to have it now that I don't have our backyard... I'll make a list and make calls tomorrow. "That sounds good. Now here let's eat some of this yummy yummy noodles and watch a movie, what do you say?" "Yes!" She clapped her hands. I grabbed our bowls, tucked 2 bottles of water in my arm and grabbed my phone and headed to the couch and settled in. My phone dinged and I grabbed it seeing it was Tim I check it immediately, "I'm okay, they just insist I stay the night to make sure I don't have another reaction. No work tomorrow for either of us. See you 10:30."   "Okay, I'll be thinking about..." I clicked the back space a lot and retyped, "I'll have breakfast ready."   Next morning at 10 o'clock I changed into a black sweat outfit and got Lila dressed in a matching pink one and got started on some pancakes and at 10:30 sharp there was a knock on the door. I opened it to see Tim in sweats and t-shirt himself. I smiled and he returned it. "Timmmm" Lila squealed jumping in his arms. "Little Boot," he scooped her up and airplane flew her to the table. "I made pancakes, I'm sure your hungry..." i slid them both plates. "Thanks." "I'm having a pink party with lightsabers!" Lila said in her little toddler voice. I smiled at her. She really is something else. She's so smart and advanced for her age. Emmetts mom paid for her to go to a private daycare before that works the kids really hard to be advanced. But she still says words super cute like, pawty and sayder.   "Ooo that will be fun!" Tim told her with a smile. "Will you come." "Of course I will! where will it be?" He asked me. "I'm not sure yet. I was going to call around today." I told him. "We can have it in my backyard." He said not leaving it up for discussion. "All done!" Lila jumped down running for the toys on the floor. "Where's Jackson?" Tim asked. "Work. We only got the day off cause you went and passed off." I teased him. "Listen, what we talked about yesterday... I meant every word but this could be bad if it gets out." He told me. "I know

Tim. And I meant every word too." "IA would for-sure have our asses if anyone even thought we were more than friends." I frowned. "I know we can separate work us and outside of work us. Like yesterday I didn't hesitate to leave your side and help them when the shooting started." I pleaded with him. "And I know you would have anyone's back out there and not just mine. No matter what. You would go for the safest save. Or the save with the better outcome." I hated to admit but I knew Tim would never risk his job. "I know, but no one else would believe it. I'm your partn... I mean TO and your career could be put at risk over this Luce. All my training gone to waste." He tried to joke but I couldn't even smile. The tears started... "How about we go in there and be honest . Cause to be truthful until yesterday I didn't realize I had the feelings I did Tim. But I knew there was something." "Me too." He sighed. "Think they will believe us?" He asked. "We never know til we try." "They could put an end to me being your TO you might have to start from the beginning.." "I know, but I'm willing to risk. I'm not saying I want anything serious right now. But I want to be able to go out to dinner or a movie or to the park with Lila and not have to hid a hand touch or putting my head on your shoulder." "I'm okay with that. I am. If your willing to risk this I am to." He grabbed my hands in his. "Let's go. Before I lose the nerve. Lila sweetie want to come with mommy to the station?" "Let's go mama!" She said. I giggled. I changed her pull up real quick and Tim, Lila and I headed to my car. The drive was quick and quiet. "Remember to tell them at work I'm just boot. Out of work who knows, friends with the possibility of becoming more." I told him. "I know Luce. Calm down."

We walked to Commander West's office and checked in with his secretary. I gave Lila her tablet and we played on it til they called Tim and I back. I grabbed her hand and I squeezed Tim's before dropping it. We both approached Commander West and stood at ease after I helped Lila sit down. "You too wish to speak to me?" "Yes sir." Tim said as I nodded in agreement. "Well go ahead." Me and Tim looked at each other and I decided to speak first. "Well Tim and I have discovered we have feelings for each other. We don't know what yet... not necessarily that we want to be boyfriend and girlfriend. But we also feel more than TO and trainee and friends." I spit out. "Interesting." He nodded as he folded his hands on his desk. "Now do either of you feel you have affected on the job by this?" "No sir." We both said. "Lucy would you be willing to take your Rookie test right now to prove that he has trained you properly?" Me and Tim looked at each other and he nodded at me in encouragement. "Yes sir." I said confidently knowing that Tim felt it helped me as well. "Very well. I assume Officer Bradford will watch the little one while you get started?" "Of course. Go ahead boot. And you got this." He said with a small smile. I nodded and smiled. "Tell mommy she's got this, Lila" Tim said picking her up. "You got this!" She held up her 2 thumbs. It handed all my belongings to them and followed Commander West to a room where a officer sat. They handed me a pencil and the test and gave me 2 hours. No breaks.

2.5 hours later

We were told to wait and once they had my score we would talk with Commander again. I was currently pacing back and forth. "What I failed? What if I didn't do good enough? What if we didn't prove to him we can be both and it not affect our job." I went on and on as Tim watched me. "Why are you smiling like that." I snapped. "Because, I know you did well. Your the best Rookie I've ever had." He said. "That's TO Tim by the way." He said with a small smile. "Your right. I need to calm down. We knew this would happen. We knew we would have to prove this legit." I sat down. And immediately got back up to pace again. "I don't think commander West will be happy if you run a rut in his lobby floor." Tim nodded at me. 30 minutes later. "Officers Chen and Bradford the Commander will see you now." "Thank you." Tim said leading the way. I carried Lila with me as she chewed on her sippy cup in my arms. "Have a seat you 2." "While you were testing I spoke to a few people. I asked several officers at Mid Willshire a few questions. They were all confident that your relationship would not affect your jobs as officers, trainee and trainer. Now that being said officer Chen you have passed your test but, I was asked not to tell you your score so that I will not be disclosing today." I looked at Tim and beamed he gave me a small smile as well. "Good job Boot." Tim nodded. "Good job mommy!" Lila clapped and I smiled at her as well. "Now I will need you both to sign these forms disclosing your relationship as well as this form stating that there is no favoritism allowed and that you both lose your jobs should that happen. But the forms are a lot more detailed." I looked at Tim and he grabbed the pens and signed both. Then Commander West gave us both a copy. "Now that, that is over. Officer Chen, as a friend of my sons I want to say I'm proud of you and congratulations on passing your training test." "Thank you Commander West." He smiled and shook his hand. "Now don't make me regret this you two." "We won't sir." Tim said and left first. "Sir, I just want to say I don't really know what these feelings are . It may be nothing it may be something I just wanted us to be honest." "I understand Officer." He smiled at me and I left with Lila as well. We spent our day off getting some pink and star wars party supplies for the party and ordering a cake with pink light sabers. At the end of the day I drove back to my apartment where Tim went to his car and Lila and I walked with him. "See you tomorrow." "See you tomorrow." "Can I do something?" He asked. I nodded. He grabbed my face gently and leaned in where he pressed his warm lips to mine and I just saw sparks. And I gave in letting my follow his. I have never felt this before. Not with any guy in high school and certainly not Tim. This is definitely going to be something.   "Woah." I said as we pulled apart. Tim looked into my eyes and I could tell he felt it too. He smiled at me. A "See you tomorrow Boot." "Goodnight Tim."   "Night little Boot." He bent down and hugged Lila.   Then, Tim got in his car and drove away. I picked Lila up and we walked to mine and West's apartment.

Lila Turns 2

1 week later. Our whole circle of friends happened to get the day off. Me and Tim have done pretty well at separating work and home life. My court hearing with Emmett went as expected , he tried saying me being a cop made me unfit mother. The court pretty much laughed at him. He gets her every other weekend, and we will split holidays. Every mother Christmas morning she will have with me as well as Easter. Luckily this year I get her first for Christmas. For her Birthday I invited Emmett to her party at Tim's which he scoffed about but will be coming. And here we are party day. "Tim, can you help me hang these streamers please?" "Sure boot. Here." He climbed on the ladder beside me holding my hip and grabbed the roll. He then climbed down and strung it across the balcony. I smiled thinking how Emmett used to make me do it all alone. I think me and Tim will progress and make a nice family. But for now this is nice. Once everything was set up Lila woke up from her nap in her pack n play I

brought with us for today. "Pawty?" She asked I nodded at her.

I picked her up took her to get changed and then we headed to Tim's backyard where Lopez, Wesley, Jackson, and Bishop waited. "Hey guys thanks for coming!" "Thank you!" Lila squealed at them causing me to giggle. "Mommy it so pwetty." She beamed with a huge smile. "Only best for you." I touched her nose. "Daddy!!" She jumped from my arms and ran to him giving him a hug. I looked at him and he looked away from me. "How's my princess?" "I miss you." She said. "I miss you too baby. You get to come stay with Daddy after your party. How's that sound?" "Good." She put a thumb up at him. I went to the kitchen to pull out the snacks and in walked Emmett. We were alone I felt my body go stiff. "So you shacking up with pretty boy now?" He asked . "No, he just let me use his yard for the party to save me from paying for a venue." I told him. "Next time ask me. She's my kid too Lucy." He told me sons got a little too close for my liking. "and I don't appreciate you prancing around with her like she's Tim's. I know everything Lucy. And I will make you pay, one way or another." I was now backed into a corner and felt trapped. "What's going in here?" Nolan came in and then Tim. "Lucy you okay?" He asked. "Yeah. He's just helping me with the food." I handed Emmett a platter of food. "Right Emmett?" "Yeah." He said and stalked off. "Here guys help me out." I handed the other men plates as well. And when they all were gone I let the tears come out. But only for a second . It is Lilas birthday and I need to strong. After everyone ate I asked Lila if she was ready to do presents. "Yes mommy!" "Here take pictures for us please Angela?" I smiled. "Of course! Here mama." She took the camera. "Smile you 2." She snapped a picture of us before the presents and then we started. She got clothes from Emmetts mom and dad. Emmett got her a Marshall fire truck. I got her dance lessons and some cute dance clothes. The neighbor said if I'm working she had no problem walking her down the road a little bit for practices. Lopez and Wesley got her a cop and lawyer Barbie. Jackson West got her a cop uniform and a light saber. Which she played with for 5 minutes before deciding to go back to her presents. She then opened a art set from Nolan. Bishop got her an outfit that made her look like baby Yoda. She loved it. And lastly Tim got her a indoor play set with a tower and slide. She was beyond excited and gave him the biggest hug. "Thank you so much everyone. To have you all here is a blessing and Lila loves everything you guys got her." She blew them all a kiss from my arms. "I'm going to go get the cake in just a few after I clean this all up." I smiled. "Here let me help." Tim said grabbing the bag and helping me collect all the paper. We stacked all the toys and clothes in the few bags the gifts were in and it all fit. I looked around and Lila was sitting with Emmett playing with her art set. "What happened earlier?" He asked me. "Nothing. It was nothing. I'm gonna go grab the cake and plates okay?" I said. "Sure I'll finish up here." He said.

I walked in the kitchen and not even a few minute later Emmett was in there again.   "Lucy, Lucy, Lucy."   "Emmett can't you just leave me alone for Lila's sake?" I snapped. "No. I want you back as my good little house wife. Not out there playing a bimbo cop. And I always get what I want." He sneered at me.   "Well good luck trying because I'm gone Emmett. You lost me." "LIKE HELL I DID." He roared shoving me into a wall where I hit my head off something hard. "Get off her." Tim came in shoving Emmett off me and into a wall. "You lay one more hand on her and you'll be fucking sorry." Tim said. "You can either leave Lucy alone the rest of the party or you can leave now and return for Lila at the end of the block when it's over. It's your choice." Tim said. "I will get you back Lucy." Emmett walked away to the backyard. "Are you okay?" He tilted my head up to inspect my eyes.   "Yeah I'm just shook up." I nodded. "Let's go the guests are waiting." I smiled. I grabbed the cake and off we went. Lila sat on my lap with Tim by my side and Emmett on the other as everyone sang Happy Birthday and then Lila blew her candles out. "What did you wish for baby girl?" "For daddy to stop hurting mommy. I saw him in the kitchen." With that Emmett stomped off and everyone looked saddened. "Let's eat cake." I smiled. "Hold on let me get a picture." Lopez said.

"Tim lean in there." She snapped the picture. "Perfect. Now we eat!" She smiled.

After cake I helped Lila get changed into shorts and a tank top and packed her clothes to come home in.   "You have fun with daddy and be a good girl okay?" I asked her.   "I want to stay with you mommy."   "I know baby but daddy misses you and wants to see you. I'll see you Monday after work."   "Okay mommy. Me wuv you." She hugged me really tight.   "If you need anything call me." I said to Emmett. "We'll be fine. Bye." He said and yanked Lila in his arms and left.   I slid down the side of Tim's house and cried. I'm scared. Emmett clearly isn't thinking right now and he has my daughter. What if he gets drunk and forgets to change her or gets mean.   "Lucy!" Angela came around "are you okay? TIM ITS LUCY!" She yelled. "I'm fine. I'm fine."   "Did he hurt you? I'll kill him." Tim said crouching down beside me. I shook my head.   "I'm scared for Lila. I don't trust him." I said.   "He won't do something stupid enough to hurt her." Angela sat down beside me. Soon everyone was out by me on the ground. Nolan brought beer. "Here." He passed one to everyone.   "Is this from my fridge boot?" Tim asked looking at the label.   "I owe you." Nolan raised an eyebrow.   "Damn right." He said.   I cried and drank. "I need something stronger." I nodded.   "Wesley got get 2 bottles of tequila, 2 bottles of jack." She looked at him.   "You got it."   "Come on Lucy. Let's go sit not on the ground beside my house." Tim said and helped me up.   "Go ahead guys we'll catch up." I nodded holding Tim back.   I pulled him into a hug and held on to him like a life raft.   "She'll be okay honey." He said running his hand soothingly on my back.   "Thank you."   "How is it that fucker gets within feet of you and you come out bruised and crying, but you can take down a 200 lb suspect in one move?"   "I don't know..." I said shaking my head.   "This angers me." He pointed to my neck from when I was pushed against the wall.   "I know... but I'm used to it." "And you shouldn't be. I shouldn't have left your side today." His nostrils flared a little bit but I wasn't scared at all. I trusted Tim 100%.   "Let's go before they miss us."

Once Wesley can back I took 3 shots of tequila with Lime and salt. And I felt so much better. Lopez matched me. "Woah." Wesley said his eyes getting huge as Lopez raised and eyebrow and smirked at him.

We all sat around and drank and everyone laughed and told stories about there rookie days or the academy but after an hour or so my mind kept going to what is Lila doing? Is Emmett watching her? I had to know...

I got up and went to the bathroom. I looked myself in the mirror and kept telling myself I needed to just relax and enjoy myself. Mirror talking/pep talks is another thing I learned in college.   But it just didn't work... I went to my car got in and started it. I went over wether I was safe or not to drive. I was fine. So, I started to drive to Emmett's but I stopped myself.

And just went home and laid in Lila's bed and cried. I don't know how I'll survive this arrangement.

Tim's POV   "Lucy's taking a while , will you go check on her Lopez? I feel clueless. I'm used to strong confident badass Lucy. Not this fragile confused Lucy..." I shook my head. I still feel like I can't live without her I just don't know how to help her. Emmett makes her weak... sorry to say and I hate him for it. I'm used to her being a cocky badass. I don't mind holding her and being there for her. I always will, she makes me caring and soft for her and I love her for that. Wait, what! I almost spit my beer out. "Um, Tim. Lucy's not in the bathroom and her cars gone." Lopez told me. "What?? She's had way too much to drink. She wouldn't do that." I said. "Well she did. But Tim she really didn't drink like us. She had those 3 shots but her bottles still full. And the one beer she asked for is half gone that's it." "Yeah I haven't drank much either I'll drive. We'll go check her apartment and we can decide from there." Wesley said. "No there's no we decide. It's me decide what to do." I said. "Tim she probably just needs some space. She's been through a lot." Lopez told me. Damn, she was right. "Why do I keep falling for girls that turn into this.. worrying and stressing." "She is not Isabel. And you knew what she was going through before you decided to tell her she meant something to you. You can't just go give up or compare her to someone she's nothing like." "She's right. Lucy's something special. She wasn't like this when she first started the academy." John told me. I took a big mouthful of beer and swallowed. "What do you mean?" "Well Lucy never cried not even when she was tazed in the academy. No she just stood up strong and walked it off." West said. My eyes got big. Even I cried. "She was confident. Much like she is when she's on a call. She held her head high. Then one day she came in and I could tell something was different." John took a drink of his beer and exhaled. "She looked in pain. But then we did a drill or practiced a stop and she seemed confident again. I blame Emmett." "Well what do you want to do?" Lopez asked. "Just make sure she's home then message me." I said to West since they live together. "Alright we're heading home. Hey, she's good for you. Makes you a better man. This will get better." She kissed my cheek then left with Wesley. "Night I'm heading out to." Nolan said.

Impact

The next morning I woke up in Lilas bed to my alarm blaring. I silenced it. Showered. Tried to eat but nothing sounded good. I grabbed my phone and called Emmett. "Hi you've reached..." I hung up. Of course no answer. Monday. Monday. Monday. It's only Saturday. "Morning." Jackson came out of the bathroom. "Morning." "You know you scared us by leaving last night and telling anyone. Especially Tim..." "I know I just couldn't handle it anymore... I needed to be home. I couldn't pretend to be okay. It felt wrong." I said. "I get it. Just next time don't give us a heart attack." "Sorry." "I'm gonna go in and blow off some steam.." I said . "See you in an hour." I threw my trainers on and jogged the 15 minutes to work. I got in and went to the gym. Where I beat on the bag til I only had 10 minutes to be at roll call. Tim comes in and sits down with the other TOs his eyes shooting me daggers I gulp. He doesn't look like Tim. My Tim. But this is our first shift since the conversation with Commander West. Maybe he's just trying too hard to be a normal TO. Sargent Grey came in and wrote 3 numbers on the board 81, 91, and 97. "All right. Shake off the rust and grab a seat. Anyone want to guess what these numbers represent? Nolan." Grey asked. "Those are the scores to our six-month exams." Know it all Nolan said. I giggled at what I thought. "That is correct, Officer Nolan." Grey pointed at him and smiled. "Oh! We all passed." I tried to act surprised knowing I had atleast passed way before now but no one else here knows that. "Technically, yes, but that 81 is ugly, given that an 80 is basically an F." Oh god... what if that's my ugly score? No it couldn't be... Commander West would never let me and Tim slide if that was me. "Who got the low mark?" Lopez asked , I'm sure her and Tim are just dying to figure out whose score is whose... but he has to have the same thought as me since he knows my test passed enough to let a TO, trainer relationship slide... right? "Clearly not West." Tim said considering Jackson was the prodigy son... golden boy West. Now for our assignment from Grey, "I could tell you, but self-reflection is necessary for your success as a patrol officer. So I want your guesses, as to which score is yours by end of shift. Understood?" "Why not give them now?" Jackson asked. He had a point, telling us would just make it easier... but then again as an officer nothing is easy. "To mess with our heads." Nolan pointed out. Which from my schooling I know is correct... sitting on stuff has a way to make reflection work out. "Are you saying you're so easily sabotaged, Officer

Nolan?" Grey asked us.   "No, sir, I was speaking for Officer Chen." He tried to make a joke. I shot him a dirty look letting him know that was NOT cool. But him and Grey both smiled. "Sir, will there be consequences for the officer with the low score?" I braved asking... not wanting to know the answer. "Officer Lopez, you want to take that?" "At a minimum, a low score means merciless taunting for months." Lopez told us. It had to be me I was nervous because of all that was at stake. Would the Commander just be okay with a passing score? "Great."   "But you three did pass, so there's good news - you can now wear short sleeves. Congratulations."   "Nolan." He answered Nolan's hand raise.   Yes no more sweating to death!!! "Sir, who will I be riding with today?" Nolan asks. "I was thinking me, how does that sound?" He holds up a thumbs up. But looks scared to death...

I go and get changed into short sleeves I see a few bruises from yesterday but ignore them and then go out to the hall to find Tim and Angela talking . I mean Bradford and Angela, I'm just boot right now.

"What are you doing?" Tim asks me once he sees me in my short sleeve uniform. "What?" I was confused.   "My rookies wear long sleeves and ties til the last day of probation boot." "Yeah but sergeant Grey said—" my smile faded as his face stayed hard and unwavering. "Grey is not your training officer. I have complete discretion of the training of my boot, and that includes uniform. Okay? So go change back into your long sleeves. And don't forget the tie." He gets impatient when I just stare at him wordlessly and says, "Now, Boot." I bump into Nolan and he asks where I'm going. "To change back."

We get in cruiser and Tim says, "that looks like one of my rookies now." "Your taking this just boot thing too far." "No this is how I treat all my Rookies. Can't play favorites Chen." I humph at him. "How is Lila?" He asked try to make small talk... I'm not in the mood but I answer anyway.. "I wouldn't know. Father of the year won't answer my calls." "Really... should we do a welfare check?" "No we can't. It's violation of our agreement..."

After a prank call we head to the park. "Stop pouting." Tim says and uses a finger to lift my chin up. "I'm not pouting, what are we doing here?" I ask. "You thought it was going to be easier after your exam. But your wrong." He tells me. I look at him and try to read him. And I fail. "Awesome." "What's that?" "Nothing" "If recent events have taught us anything, it's that we need to remain ever-vigilant. You probably think you know everything about policing, but you don't. For example, what's the most important thing you need on the street?" Tim asked me. "Is this a trick question? Okay, well, the easy answer is my gun, but I know that's not right. So, my mind? No. That's too esoteric for you." I quip back. "Are you done not answering my question?" He asks.

What would it be, what would it be? Judgement! "Uh my, judgement? Yeah my judgement!" I said unsure what Tim Bradford would say or think.

"Your eyes. "Cop eyes" stop crime and save lives. Did you study explosive devices in the Academy?" He asked. Explosives? What! We did but it definetly was a big part of our studies. "What? Yeah a little." I told him. "Good. I hope you paid attention because I had a buddy from the bomb squad mock up an IED and hide it somewhere here in this park." He told me.... What!! "What." I said annoyed. What in the hell Tim. We are wasting time here ! "You got 10 minutes to find it, or I'm adding the duty hat to your standard uniform. Go." Oh no that things terrible. No no no. "Go 10 seconds!" I start looking around the park... I walk around. Cops eyes on. Four minutes in is when I see a blinking green in garbage can I run to it. "I found it. I found–" and it explodes white stuff all over my uniform. I grimace. "And you're dead. Because radio frequency energy can trigger a bomb. You gonna forget that lesson, Boot?" "No." I said... "Good. Go get cleaned up." I get cleaned up and go to find Tim. "Tim we need to talk." "If it's about the lesson Lucy save it." "No it's about last night..." "Go on." He crosses his arms and looks at me. "I'm sorry I left without telling anyone. I know that's what this is about.." "No this is about the second part of your training Lucy." "Seriously Tim, turn off TO Tim for one minute please." "Fine." "You need to learn to gain your confidence back." "I have it." "No you have it now, at work. When you get off it's all going to go away again. Like yesterday." "Tim..." "No don't try and argue it, it's true." "Fine maybe it is. But what does blowing up baby powder in my face going to do about it." "Nothing. I just want to make sure you don't get blow up one day because you use a radio by a bomb." "Fine." I humph. "One last thing." "Yes?" He asks. "Long sleeves still, really?" "Yes I really do make my rookies wear them longer Grey knows it. Can't treat you different can I boot? Let's go. We got work to do." When back in the cruiser I tried Emmett again to get no answer... he's the worst . He knows this is driving me crazy... he still can get in my head and we're not even together anymore.

We were soon dispatched to a missing persons call. Tim and I knocked on the door. The guy who answered the door seemed distraught. He told us they were trying to have a baby and that his wife was supposed to come home to try. When Tim asked for a picture he started to show us one on his phone but Tim told him a hard copy was better so he went to get one. "Poor guy." I said. "Really?" Tim bit back. "What." I said. "Cop eyes." He pointed to his eyes. I rolled mine. "What you think the husband did something?" "You always think the husband did something. Your not the first woman to get abused by her man..." ouch low blow. What the hell is wrong with him today. "Officer Bradfords first rule of domestics?" I tried joking and he was not having it. "This isn't a joke, Boot. You don't have the experience to evaluate people yet, so your default should be suspicion, not compassion. Understood?" "Yeah."

When we head back to the shop I huff. "What?" "Nothing." I try calling Lila again and no answer. "Lucy." "Emmett still isn't answering my calls." "Lucy, you need to focus." "You know as well as I do once we're on a call or patrolling My eyes are open so stop treating me like I'm incompetent. Do you really think if I almost failed Commander West would have been okay with this?" "7-Adam-19 requesting back up at a fire the i-96 over pass." "7-Adam-19 put us in route." I say back as Tim heads where we need to be. We go to the call but there isn't much for us to do. I catch up with Jackson and Nolan who are scared of being the ones with the low grade. But with what Tim put me through today I'm sure it was me.

At the end of the call we head back to the Sally Port where Tim get out of the shop and heads for the exit. "What are you doing?" I ask him. I need to know what I did so wrong. "Clocking out and heading home Rio Bravos on cable." He states. "No, no. Why are you treating me like it's day one all over again?" I ask. "Because it is. Today was day one of your second stage of training." He says as if it is so obvious and that anyone can tell what Tim Bradford is thinking. "So what does that mean I've lost all the respect that I've earned?" I asked tossing my hands in the air. "You lost that when you lied on a report." What?! "What?" I say out loud after staring at him for a few seconds. "I read your account of what happened at the quarantine house." "O-Okay?" I'm still not understanding. "When I thought I was infected, I told you I'd rather take my life than bleed out. You failed to report it." "That's what this is about?" "Suicide ideations by a law enforcement officer are extremely serious and should have been reported immediately." "I was trying to protect you. They would have put you on leave, required therapy. You weren't even actually suicidal." He really wasn't. If he was going to die a slow painful death he was going to do it on his own terms and quick. "Not your call! You should have detailed everything, regardless of the consequences." He got close to me... I could feel his breath. "Lucy, if anyone found out about our agreement with The Commander and that you lied about something like that, our careers would be over." I swallowed. "Tim I didn't think about that.. I just knew that because of the situation is the only reason you would ever say something like that. You are far from suicidal..." "I know but what we have makes us have to cover our asses 10x more than anyone else here does." "I'm sorry." "It's fine go get changed. Your coming over tonight." "Oh so I'm more important that Rio Bravo now?" I wiggle my eyebrows. "Go. Before I change my mind."

I went to the showers and took one. I left my hair down and threw on my black stretchy shorts and my long sleeve gray shirt that says LAPD down the arm. I then grabbed my bag and met Tim at his car.

We drove to his house in silence I messed with his radio and chose songs to annoy him just because I can right now. It didn't work. I huffed again.   "You know you've huffed more times today than even I have in my whole career." He told me... he's not wrong today has just been orating. The scores, Grey's mind test, my uniform shirt, the baby powder... the list goes on...   "It's just what you said earlier at the missing persons call got under my skin. And Emmett not answering that's not helping." "I'm sorry... I just was being rough because I'm sure you don't want to believe that , that could have been you..." "It would never be me... you would have knew something was up and been on my trail within hours... I'd never just be missing and forgotten. I couldn't even miss a day of work without you knowing something was up." We pulled into Tim's and walked to his door. We got in and he looked at me. He lifted my chin and check my bruise from yesterday out. "I hate that I wasn't there sooner."   "I know." He still had me pinned by the door. He leaned in and kissed the bruise gently. My breath hitched. "Tim..." "Do you want me to stop?' He kissed my jaw this time.   "No." His lips moved closer and closer till he touched my lips. I kissed him with so much intensity. I saw fireworks and felt heat in places I haven't felt heat in, in a long time. "Tim I... I need you."   "Are you sure?" I nodded and started to pull his shirt off and he let me. We kept kissing and grabbing at each other with lust and ecstasy til we made it to his room.

The next morning I woke up wrapped in Tim's sheet. I rolled over and was met with an empty bed but I heard noise coming from his bathroom that was connected the bedroom. I got up slowly and found my shorts and shirt discarded in the hall and pulled them on. Making my way to his kitchen where I found a pot of coffee and poured one for myself. I started sipping my coffee and remembering last night. A few minutes later I heard Tim's footsteps. "Morning." "Good morning." I smiled. "Yes it is." He poured his own cup of coffee. "Im sorry you missed Bravo Rio." I joked with him and he laughed. "I recorded it, last night was so much better than what I had originally planned." He laughed and came up behind me kissing his cheek. I smiled. Last night was so much different than what I was used to with Emmett. Emmet was all things Tim is not. Emmet was rough and greedy where as Tim was gentle and very giving. Emmett was the first person I was ever with, I never knew sex felt this good... "What's wrong?" Tim asked turning around from the fridge with a carton of eggs, "are you hungry?" I nodded. "Nothings wrong." "Well you went from smiling like a bubbling idiot to frowning in seconds." "Last night was just something I never experienced... being with you was so different." "Oh really?" He looked kind of offended. "In a good way I promise." I reassured. "Well I would hope." We chit chatted while Tim made breakfast and we ate together. But before it was over we ended up back in his room. After our pre-work workout we laid in each others arms. "What are we?" I asked, we never established each other as talking, boyfriend and girlfriend... nothing. "Well we definitely are more than friends." He said. "Well yeah, friends don't do this." I gestured to our naked bodies pressed together. "Lucy Chen, will you be my girlfriend?" "Hmmmm..." I said teasing him with a smile. "Yes I will be."

"Tim we got to be at work in like 30 minutes." I told him as we laid wrapped in each others arms. "I know. I only live 10 minutes away." "I need to go shower." I kissed his lips and made it to his bathroom where I took a fast shower and changed into the set of clothes I had in my bag, Jean shorts, a tank top and a thin flannel. I liners my hair up in a bun and headed to the car where Tim waited. "Tim... what will people think?" I asked realizing we would be pulling into work when other people are... there was already chatter about us but this would set it over the top. "Do you really care?" I shook my head. "No. Do you?" "Would I be doing this?" We made it to work with enough time to both change and make it to the briefing room.

Sitting in the briefing room I was chatting with Nolan about our guess as West comes up. "Uh-oh. Looks like somebody's stressed about their test scores." "Yeah, well, we both think we got the 91." I told j. "Which means one of us got the 81." I know it wasn't me... I just can't break it to him. "All right, take your seats. As expected, the stolen uniforms caused a bit of paranoia out there. Overnight, there were two fights and a near shooting 'cause two officers didn't recognize each other. All right, that being said, it is vital that we remain vigilant. Understood? Now, to your exam scores. You all submitted your guesses last night, and none of you guessed right." Grey came in and announced to us all.

"Thank God." I said loud enough to earn a few chuckles, I then turned to John and said, "Nolan, I'm sorry." Trying to be nice but I think it was more...   "Save your concern, Officer Chen. Officer Nolan got the highest score, not the lowest. That "honor" goes to Officer West." "That's not possible." And she is not wrong, WHAT?!?! Golden boy?

"I've seen a lot of strange things in my 20 years, but never would I have imagined that the golden boy would tank his test." Yeah he got that right. Strange it is.   "But there's a th- like, I-I -" West was just staring ahead and stuttering, I felt bad I really did.

"Uh-oh. Looks like Grey broke your rookie." Tim told Lopez.   "Shut up." She snapped as Russo appears in the doorway. "Ah, Agent Russo. You looking for me?" Grey asked. "No. Actually, Officer Nolan. Can you spare him for the morning? I need his help running down a lead. He nods at Nolan and then dismisses us all to work.

I head to the kitchen where I find a still stunned West. "Are you okay?" "Yeah fine. It's not like it's the first time I didn't get the highest score." He is a terrible liar. "Dude." "Look, after the terrorist on the bus, I just needed a little bit of time off. I figured I knew this stuff backwards and forwards, but clearly, that was a mistake. Clearly, I should have kept studying." It really did mess with me too. But I still studied... "Jackson-" he cut me off, "look, I let everyone down." "West your cadets are here." He walked out without even saying bye.

I head to the stairwell where I find another man in uniform but he looks a little confused. "Hold that, please." I grab the door before it closes. "Oh. Yeah." I say and hold it. "Thanks." He says. "Yeah, no problem." I nod. The man goes over to a police unit and peers through its window. This is weird... I've never seen another cop act like this. "Hey, are you looking for something?" I ask him getting a little antsy and weirded out. "Oh, yeah, um, my wallet." He says. "Ah." Makes sense but I still find his behavior odd and continue to assess the situation with my cop eyes. I move behind another vehicle and watch as he takes something out of one of the units. "Did you find it?" I ask. "Yeah. Thanks. Yeah." He was being short and defiently sounds... woah why does he have a radio and equipment?

"What are you doing with that radio?" And the man flees on foot. "Hey! Stop! 7-Adam-19, chasing a fake cop in the garage. I need backup. Hey! Stop!" The man leaps over the side of the garage level and I look down as he lands in a dumpster below. He scrambles out and I drops down after him, but he jumps in a car before i can catch him. I climb out and call off the back up and tell them he got away. Grey had me meet him up back in the parking garage. We were standing by the ledge we jumped from.   "And you jumped from here?" He pointed at the ledge.   "Yes sir."   "Are you okay?" He scans over me. "Yeah." I said getting a little annoyed with the 21 questions about the jump. "You went right over after him?" Tim walks up and says, "of course she did I trained her." He smiled widely as he said it... proud almost. "Mm-hmm your saying this guy stole a radio?" Grey finally asked a non-annoying question. "Yes, sir, out of Car 26. Actually, he he wasn't wearing gloves. Maybe we can pull a print?" I suggested.   "Great idea Officer Chen. Why don't you practice that while I talk with Officer Bradford." I smiled and headed to get a dusting kit. I pulled the print and had it sent to forensics.   I went in the kitchen and tried Lila again... no answer. I'm getting annoyed now. All these thoughts in my head.. not knowing what's going on. "Let's go boot." I follow Tim to the shop. I get in, fasten my belt and we are off on patrol. "What did Grey want?" "He just asked about what was going on with us and about what Commander West said." "And?" "He agrees that he thinks we are able to separate the two." "Good." Then a call comes over the police scanner warning us to stop a evidence transportation that was hijacked by the fake cops. We can't radio in a signal because they are jamming the signal.

We find the transportation, "there it is. Fake transports already got them." I shake my head this is nuts, impersonating a cop is just foolish.   "Can't warn the truck driver, because our heist crew's jamming the signal with their stolen radio."

"Shouldn't we wait for back up?" I ask him. "We are the back up." He tells me. I take a deep breath. Tim pulled the shop where we were blocking the road the convoy was on. "Come on get ready, and remember they don't know we know." He said looking at me. I nodded and we get out of our shop. "What's the problem?" The fake cop asks us. "Radios are down and we were sent to escort the truck back to the courthouse." Tim said confidently. I noted that the fake cop had his vest on the outside of his uniform. "Must be a mistake cause we're the escort so get out of the way." He said. "No problem we were headed to lunch when we got the call." As we headed back to the car I saw another person in the back of the car with a very large non cop looking firearm. "Tim?" There's no way he missed that... the way he hammers cop eyes in my head. "Yeah I see it." He whispers to me. "One last thing before we go. Real cops wear there vest under there shirts." A shoot out starts I grab a smoke bomb and throw it into the line of fire. Man I love this job. I use the distraction to get behind the man with large gun. Lopez and West pull in taking care of another unit of fake cops. I notice Mr. Big staring Tim down still. I'm not having that.   "Drop your weapon right now! Down on the ground, facedown, hands apart! Don't you move." As I'm saying this I use a little force to get him down and cuffed. "Up." I pull him a little to get him to his feet.

We get back the precinct where I start paperwork and Tim does his. I down a bottle of water. Once all my paperwork's done I hand it to Tim to look over who nods. "Good work today." "Thanks." I grab my phone and try to call Lila again. No answer. "Hey let me do you a favor. As Tim not your TO." "Officer Michaels!" He yells. "Can you do a welfare check for me?" "Sure." Tim writes an address down. "What exactly am I checking on." "Her kid. Her ex isn't answering has a little violent side, used to have a PFA on him. Not answering anyone. Just want to make sure the kids okay." "He's a drinker too." I pipe in. "And not a light drinker." "Okay. I'll give you call when I'm done." "Thanks we owe you." I say. "Thanks Tim. I'm going to head home tonight." "See you in the morning?" I nod.

False Alarm

It's Monday after shift today I get to go get Lila. Tim's friend called and let him know that Emmett did answer the door and that Lila appeared to be okay though he didn't let him get close. But to know he didn't flee with her was good.   I got in the shop and Tim passed me a book. "If I have to suffer, so do you. So, you're gonna read this out loud to me between calls. Only way I'm gonna get it memorized in time." Tim has been working on becoming a Sargent and they added 2 more books to the list.   "It I could drive and you could read it to yourself." I told him.   "Nice try. Start reading Luce." "Okay. "Chapter One. True leadership generates respect, not fear. It elevates people, rather than diminishing them." I like this book." "You would. Keep reading." He told me.   ""The number-one mistake new leaders make is to think themselves suddenly infallible. The best leaders understand that even the lowliest patrol officer has something valuable to teach them." Repeat that last part back to me. Memorizing is all about repetition. Trust me. I'm a psych major. I know this stuff." He repeated it back just fine. "Again." Then we were dispatched to a family disturbance on Evergreen. Tim was definitely delighted. "7-Adam-19, copy. En route. Okay, ETA three minutes. Time to read some more. "An open mind and an open door." When we arrive on scene we are met with 2 Morons who are trying out military vests. Once they shook it appeared they were both okay but we were wrong and 1 of them was hurt. So we had to call an ambulance.

Once back in the shop and on patrol Tim has me read to him again. A little ways in I tell Tim he's just gonna have to re read it to really memorize it. "No. I memorize best when I hear it." "Really?" "Yeah." "Huh." This sounds like a learning difference I learned about in psych school. "Why?" "Nothing." "Boot." "You might have a learning difference." I don't like the word disability for this type of learning difference. "A what?" He asks me. I look at his face and he looks confused, that's a look I've never seen on Tim Bradford before. "Technically, it's classified as a disability, but it really just means that you're wired to process information differently. In your case, through through hearing rather than reading." I explained it to him. "I don't have a learning disability." He defended himself. "A lot of people have them. I bet Isabel helped you in the Academy, read through the materials with you and stuff." I tried to make him feel better. "We're not talking about this." We were then dispatched to a call. I had thought to record his books for him.

When we get to the call Tim seems to know the guy, Rex, he's a bonds man out to get a dangerous man. "You know as Tim, I like seeing you get brave like that... take charge." "Oh really?" I ask raising an eyebrow. "Yes really..."

Later that night... I went to Emmett's to get Lila. I knocked on the door. "What. Here to see if I'm being a dad okay?" "Well you weren't answering and I was scared for our daughter. Where is she?" I looked around him and didn't see her. "LILA!" He yelled a little harsher than I liked. Soon I heard her foot steps. "Mommy!" She jumped in my arms. "We go home?" "Yes baby." I turned to Emmett and asked for her stuff. "Here's your shit by the way." He threw a whole box open in the yard and slammed the door. I say Lila down and worked on picking it all up. I heard the door open again and he came back out. "By the way bitch, I don't have to answer your calls. Send the police here again for no reason and you'll regret it. Do you hear me?" "You know what Emmett. I'm sick of you treating me this way... like I'm nothing. I am something, I am the mother of that beautiful little girl. All I wanted was to talk to her." "Well guess what when she's with me, she's not your fucking problem." He got close to me. "Yes she is. She's always my PRIORITY." I emphasized that word because my Lila is the farthest thing from a problem. "Oh really? Then why are you a cop Lucy? All you have to do is stop being a cop and you can come home. I'll stop being this asshole you've made me become." He had me backed into the house. He wrapped his arm around me and grabbed my butt way too hard. It hurt. "That hurts stop." "No, I miss this ass. Maybe I'll get a taste." He bent down and kissed my neck. "Mommy!" Emmetts head snapped up and he turned around I took that moment to duck away from him. Leaving the clothes on the ground I grabbed the box and Lila and ran for my car.   I put Lila in her seat and kissed her forehead and hauled ass home.   "Hey baby. Are you okay?" I ask hugging her tightly.   "Yes mommy." I look at her arms and her legs. And she looks okay.   "Did you eat?" "Yes mama." She said. "Movie?" "Sure. Baby, want some popcorn?" She nodded. So I grabbed some popcorn and put it in the microwave. I put in Harry Potter. Jackson came in and was stoked to watch Harry Potter with us. We settled in on the couch. I grabbed Tim's book and moved to the arm chair once Lila fell asleep and started recording it.

The next day Tim and I followed up on Rex. Who we found down. We then helped catch Nico and let him have his bounty. Later that night before we went home I went looking for Tim and found him in the gym beating on a bag. "Training for the rematch with Nico?" I joked thinking about how Nico took him down and I was there to have his back. I wouldn't want it any other way. lol "Ah, we got him in the end." I hand him an audio drive with earbuds. "Here." "What's this?" He asks. "It is Split Second Leadership: Leading Men In The Line of Duty, the audio book." I told him. "This books out of print there's no audio book." "Yeah, which is why I recorded one for you.

Uh, listen, I talked to Isabel, and from what she said, it's clear you're a kinesthetic learner, which just means that you need to listen while you're being active in order to absorb things. There's no shame in it. Really. Honestly, it's probably why you excel at being a cop. I'll see you tomorrow." "Yeah. Thanks Luce." He pulls me in for a goodnight kiss puts the earbuds in and goes back to his workout.

A few days goes by and Lila and I have had dinner with Tim once. But when she's home I make sure we come home every night. Once on shift and in the sally port Tim told me I was driving. A little bit into the shift we are dispatched to a convenience store. "What's Amari?" Tim must know the guy. "Man, this fool took a counterfeit $100 without even checking it." I took the bill he was holding out and read the hundred was spelled wrong . Tim got the guys description and we put out a BOLO before leaving.

Once we went outside Tim looked at me. "You should've gloved up when you touched the counterfeit bill in case we needed to pull prints." He told me. "You're right. Um, I spaced. I'm sorry." I paused... he usually corrects me in front of people. "Wait. Why didn't you say anything when we were inside?" "No reason." He's lying... I know when he lies. "You always call me out, in front of people when I screw up. First you let me drive, now this? Why are you being nice to me today?" I ask him... He always treats me like any other officer at work. "I'm not." "Just because I told you what happened with Emmett at Lilas pick up... Tim your breaking your own rule... you can't treat me different." "There's no rule about being nicer... it's not special treatment. But if it makes you feel any better I'm driving." "Wait, but." He was in the car so I followed. "Do you think it's stupid I'm letting it bother me." "No, I think what he did is stupid. And after seeing that handprint on you. I have half a mind go leave a mark on him." "Tim." I say sternly telling him to calm down. "I know I'm sorry. Can I tell you I'm glad you had it in you to push him away? Your getting your confidence back and I'm proud of you." "Tim pull over now." He pulls over and open the door and hurl. I close the door after wiping my mouth with my sleeve. "Sorry.... I.. the heat gets to me." I said. "It's okay... here." He grabs a napkin for the console. "Thanks." A few seconds later "hey up ahead." "That's the counterfeit guy!" I say excited to find him. Tim pulls out in front of him to block his path so I am able to apprehend him. "Hey! Hands on the hood. Let's go. All right. Spread your legs apart." Just as I'm cuffing him our phones let out a siren noise. I look at him in shock. People start running around saying the need to leave. "What do we do?" I ask him scared. "Let him go we got to get back to the station." I release the guy and we haul ass back to the station. "But Tim, Lila. I need to be with her." "We'll go back get orders and see what's going on. If this is real I promise she won't be without us." I nod. We get to the station where it is confirmed that this is not a drill. I look at him. He pulls me in for a kiss and I return it. There's so much chaos around us I don't think anyone noticed.   "Let's go get Lila." He said. "We will still need to work but we can take it easy okay." I nod at him.   "13 minutes" "Stop checking the time." We pull up to the apartment and I go to the sitters apartment. "Are you serious? We're about to be burned up by a giant fireball." I told him.   "A," no, we're not. It's a false alarm. And, "B," counting down the minutes wouldn't accomplish anything, even if it was real." He told me...

Lilas sitter opened the door, "Considering everything I need to take Lila with me." "Sure sweetie." "You should go be with your sister down the hall. If this blows over I'll bring her back there okay." "Yeah. Hey Lucy, your a good mom." "Thanks." While I was getting Lila, Tim went to my apartment and grabbed the extra car seat and I met him at the shop where it was installed. I strapped Lila in and kissed her forehead. "You want to come work with mommy and Tim today?" "Yes. Yay." She clapped her hands and squealed excited. We were dispatched back to Amari's store. So Tim had me sit with Lila while he checked it out. After a few minutes he came back. "Come on were gonna hide out here." He said. I nodded. Grabbing Lila we went back to the store. Tim glanced at his watch. "Busted. How much time we got left?" I asked. "Enough." He goes over to the liquor cabinet and grabs some whiskey taking a swig. He offers me the bottle. "I'm not a whiskey girl." I grab a bottle of tequila. Still holding Lila close to me. And take a swig. "To the end of the w-o-r-l-d" I spell it as to not scare Lila. "Here baby." I hand her a bag of m&ms. "Whenever that may be." We clink bottles and drink again. "Tim." Lila reaches for him. "Hey sweetie." He takes Lila and holds her. "I love you very much, you know that?" "Mmhmm." She says. I feel tears well in my eyes. "What's wrong mommy." "Nothing baby. I love you guys." We hold each other right. "Attention all units: missile alert is a false alarm. I repeat missile alert is a false alarm." Grey's voice rings out. "Oh thank god." I smile and kiss Lilas cheek then I lay one on Tim's lips next. "Let's get you back to your babysitters baby." "Aweee." I laugh at her little lip.

Not, Nolan

I'm sitting in the breakfast eating and man it's just not settling right... I feel super tired even though me and Lila both slept fine last night.   I hear John babbling on about something with his girlfriend being pregnant...   "Oh- I'm sorry are- are you talking to me?" I asked "What's going on?" West asks.   "Roll call." He said looking kind of down.   "Is everything alright?" l asked him.   "100%." He didn't look to positive but I let it go caught up in trying not to hurl my breakfast. I grabbed a coffee refill before heading to the briefing room.   "Okay listen up. Why is community policing important? Officer Chen?" Grey was speaking to us now in roll call. I'm seated right up front as usual with Nolan and West. Damn rookie seats.   "Uh, because it builds trust between the police and the public, leading to a reduction in crime." I answered confidently.   "Exactly. And today, we're gonna do a little trust-building. Officer Nolan, so, you know Dr. Sawyer at Shaw Memorial?" He asked .   "Uh, we went to the same college, sir. Before I got my now-ex pregnant with my son and-" come one Nolan!! "It was a yes or no question, Nolan." I chuckle at Grey always messing with Nolan.   "Sorry, sir. Yes, I know her." "Good. She requested an officer to assist with a seminar. You're going." Grey told him. "What kind of seminar?" He asked Grey.   "Don't know, don't care. Whatever it is, it's open to the public, which means you have a chance to show the community that the LAPD does more than just lock up people."   "We do?" Tim asked causing an uproar of laughter. I looked back and smiled at him and gave me little grin back.   "That's not funny. And you don't want to piss me off, Bradford. Considering what I have lined up for you." He smirks evilly. I raise an eyebrow. "What's that?" He sat forward in his seat a little.   "Watts Rams need additional coaches for their fall clinic, and you're gonna need company. Officer West. Your dad is always bragging how you're a high-school football star. Is he lying?" Grey says now. Okay what am I doing today then?   "No, sir. All-State safety, four years running. I could actually pull up my highlight reel if you want to check it out. It's on my YouTube channel." Golden boy I roll my eyes again. "That won't be necessary. Change into your PTs, head out with Bradford. Harper and Chen, you will serve as liaisons to the Mid-Wilshire Community Council. They're coming in for a sit down." I groaned.   "What is this? The 1950s? The boys go to football practice while us girls attend a PTA meeting?" Harper always with the equal rights. I look back at her and smile she raises an eyebrow.   "Fair point. Guess there's really only one way to settle this - Challenge coins."   Everyone crowds around a table where Bradford and Harper place their challenge coins down and brag about their coins.   "What is a challenge coin?" Nolan asked West.   "How do you not know that? It's a medallion bearing an organization's insignia, given only to those deemed worthy. They're used to show respect or, uh, settle minor disputes." West said to Nolan. But I wasn't sure either.   "Okay. Closest to the edge wins."

Harper won but let Tim go anyway to the football thing. I soon figured out her reasoning was that the meeting would have the lowest interference with our usual day. But, she made me do the talking boy was she wrong. I pretty much told them our task force would help with all there issues and after a while they started to realize that I was letting them hear what they wanted. So now here we are, in a sewage full of rats with a rancid smell looking for squatters. I stopped and threw up. Man what is wrong with me.

"You alright there boot?" Harper asked. "Yeah this heat has just been getting to me." "Uh huh." She said.   I caught a smell of burnt donuts from a plastic oven.   "Uh, it smells like burned donuts from a plastic oven. That's definitely meth." She examined a discarded pipe.   "The pipes still warm be on the look out."   "Behind you!" The guy took me down and Harper got him down.   "Hook him up." Soon another one came and

Harper took him down too.   "I take that back said earlier. Community meetings are all your good for."

Later we are outside the storm drain.   "Something on your mind?" She asked. "No ma'am." I lied. I want to tell her she's wrong and that I'm good at what I do.   "Yeah that's what I thought." She said all cocky. And I couldn't hold it in anymore. "Your wrong about me." "Uh, no I'm not." She said. "I can do so much more than just community meetings."   "You're right. You're probably really good at paperwork. But you can't fight and your pregnant."   "Um no I'm not. And I can fight. I've gone toe-to-toe with plenty of suspects and won." "Not that one. And we'll see." She said nodding at the guy. "He's huge!" I told her he is defiently like 5 of me.   "And yet, I took him and his buddy. You want to hit me right now, don't you? Yeah, I see it in your eyes. Someone a little more your size. Well, come on." She taunted. "Hit me, not Nolan that's an order." She said angrily.   "Do it for real!" I tried to swing at her but I didn't put my all in it. "Come for me like that tweaker came for you!" I came at her and she had me down. "Now! Aah! Stay down, and get used to that position. Because in case you didn't know, you are not a 6'2", 180-pound man. Now, Tim might be a good T.O., but he can't teach you how to fight like a girl. We get a higher show of force, especially from men. So, guess what, sweetheart? You are always going to be tested, and when you are alone against a desperate suspect, and you are between them and freedom, your thoughts can never be, "Oh, my, he's bigger than me." Look here, Not Nolan, if you're going to survive these streets as a 5'6" woman and one of color, no less, you better learn what these boys don't know to teach. And like I said if I were you I'd buy myself a pregnancy test. I know the signs and your showing them." I choked on the water I was drinking... "Tired. What have you been drinking 4-5 cups of coffee a day? Nauseous. Boobs look a little bigger." She gave me the Harper look and walked away.

We then went to our squirrel feeders residence. Who was missing 2 fingers AND had red hair. This jogged Harpers memory of the 2009 pipe bombing. Before we left the residence she had to check the garbage for samples to send in to match with the fingers on scene of the bombing. I played distraction for it. That was a big mistake.

Here I am trapped on IED pressure plates and he has gotten away. "No. Harper, don't come inside the house. It's booby-trapped. No, stay! Don't come in. It's rigged." I told her. "Where's Bosk?" "In the back room. He's arming a bomb, a big-ass bomb. You got to get clear of the house, radio the bomb squad, and clear the neighborhood. Mr. Bosk, you don't need to do this." "Why not? I'm caught. Might as well go out with a bang." "How long ago did you rig the house? Months? Years?" I asked him trying to calm him down and slowly very slowly inching a little closer to him. "Almost a decade. I've been waiting that long for cops to show up on my doorstep." He said. Wow a decade of hiding and fear... I couldn't imagine it. "A decade. Avoiding pressure plates. --" I was finally close enough and I pointed my gun at him. "Let go of the wire slowly. Turn around. Hands behind your back. Do it now!" I told him still holding the gun up to him. "Don't you want me to disarm the bombs before you cuff me?" He asked. "Nope. My guess is you'd enter a code that would set it all off. So we're going out the window." I told him and out the window we went. "Hey." Harper said "Uh, house is still booby-trapped, but he didn't finish rigging the fertilizer bomb, so-" I updated her on the call and information. "Nice work." She told me. "You got him?" I asked. "Uh-huh. Yeah." "All right." "You gonna puke?" She asked. "No. No. No. Maybe." And I threw up again.

Back at the precinct I ran into Harper.

"Hey. Nice working with you today." It really was nice to get a woman's view at policing. "Yeah, you, too. Look, I was wrong to discourage you today. Go as far as you want in this job. You say you want to be a cop like me, screw that. Be better than me. You got what it takes, Not Nolan. And hey, your secrets safe with me. But don't wait too long to find out." "I heard you call me Chen back at the house. I know you know my name. Um would it be all right if I asked you for advice, from time to time?" "Sure. Just not too often. I don't want to mess up the whole lone wolf persona I got going on." She said.

Later that night I was laying on the couch with Lila watching the next Harry Potter, we were on a kick. When I realized I did in fact miss my period a few days ago... "Ice cream?" I asked her. She just nodded to entranced in the movie. "Hey West! Tim." I said stopping wide eyed. "I invited Tim over for some Harry Potter figured you wouldn't mind?" "No not at all. I was actually just getting us ice cream..." "Ice cream for dinner?" He asked. "Well... it sounded good." "Sooo how was your day." "Good it was nice to play some ball. And a drug bust was cool too. And you?" He asked. "Eh, you know I caught the 2009 pipe bomber and almost got blown up." I said casually. Man this life is exciting. "Bad ass." We knuckle punched. "Tiiiiimmmmm!" Lila ran in and jumped in his arms. "Well hello little boot." "We gonna eat ice cream cause mommy's sad I have to go see daddy tomorrow night." I frowned a little at that. "Well how about I eat some ice cream with you guys?"He grabbed 2 spoons and handed one to Lila. And then did the same with the bowls. "What did miss Lila do today?" He asked. "I colored a picture." "Oh really? Can we see?" Lucy asked. "Yes!" She ran to her book bag and grabbed it out. There was 3 stick figures and a red sun. "And whose that?" "Me, you and Tim." "Awe baby I love it." "Me too mommy." She clapped. And I hung it on the fridge. We laid on the couch and watched the movie. And West took the love seat. "Hey she's asleep." I whispered to Tim. "Yeah, want me to move her for you?" I nodded. He picked her up in his arms and carried her to bed . And I couldn't help but smile at how great they look together. My 2 worlds.   "Night West." "Night guys." He went to his room. "Well I'm going to head home." He said. "No you can stay."   "Are you sure? I know you were nervous about confusing Lila." He out his hands on my hips loosely. "I'm sure. I know your not going anywhere." I wrapped my arms around his shoulders and pulled him in to me. "No I'm not." He pressed his forehead to mine and looked in my eyes. I pressed a kiss on his lips and he pulled us to my room.

Fraud say what?

I walk out of my room and find West steaming his class As. "Coffee?" "I haven't had a chance to make it." He says. "So, no coffee?" Lila then comes out of her room piggy tails lopsided and a stuffed animal in arm. "Ceweal?" She asks "Not yet. Sorry." "So no cereal and no coffee?" I ask "Nope." West keeps ironing. "You know, Nolan kept me up all night from this crime scene he was babysitting. Look at this. Look." I show him several selfies Nolan sent to my phone. "I thought Tim kept you up." "Shut it." I look at Lila she didn't hear that. "Yeah, he was texting me, too. We'll get stuck on one soon enough." He told me. I look down at his uniform, "Class A's?" I ask. "Yeah. Tim and I get our commendation today." He says proudly. "Oh, right, for helping that family a few weeks ago." I say. "Mm-hmm. You know, it's it's crazy. Like, a few weeks ago, I thought I was gonna get bounced from the program, and now I'm getting an award from the Deputy Chief." "It's pretty cool how quickly things can change. I'm really happy for you, man." "Aww. Thanks. Plus, Tim is gonna be in a really good mood today." "I know. I'm really happy for me, too." I reach for a carton of milk and finds it empty, gives WEST a "Really?" look. "Sorry." "Let's go get dressed baby then we'll get donuts on the way to daddy's." Dropping Lila off was pretty uneventful considering Emmett was half asleep. He mumbled a see you Sunday. And slammed the door in my face.

The last visit drop off was very similar and I'm actually glad he's leaving me alone. I took a pregnancy test a few weeks ago and am pregnant ... with Tim's baby. I'm not ready to tell him though. If I am it's only a few weeks. I'm not ready to tell anyone. Not even Nyla who tipped my clueless ass off.

"It is a big deal. "Light of the City" award? I thought you'd be happier. I planned my emotional day around it." "I don't do this for the medals and plaques, Boot." "Yes, only lesser cops enjoy recognition. But, I for one am proud of you." "Exactly." He ignored my last comment. "Well, if it doesn't matter, turn it down." I told him. Making another cup of coffee. "It doesn't matter to me, but it does matter to the higher-ups. Look, a good score on the sergeant's exam, this award could help me rise through the list of candidates." He told me... oh yeah he's going to be leaving me... at work that is. We have fallen into a partner relationship instead of TO and trainee unless I really need it. "Fair enough." I nod. "Jackson's dedicated an entire shelf to his award?" He laughed. "He's building a cabinet from scratch." I give him a scared look.   "He knows how to do that?" Tim is now laughing pretty hard I'm guessing imagining pretty boy Jackson doing that.   "Nolan's helping him." "Makes sense... but the thought was hilarious." "Oh, hey, 3:00. Skateboarder's about to grab that woman's bag." I say pointing.   The skateboarder rides innocently past the woman.   "Swing and a miss." Tim chuckles and looks at the skateboarder. I look forward and we are about to hit a vehicle. "Tim!" But he was too late we hit the back of the car.   "Woah, your bleeding." I reach up to touch it.   "I'll be fine. Are you okay." He looks me over pretty well.   "Yeah." I nod.   "Get the flares out. Seal off the whole street." He told me.   I went and blocked the street off.   Soon the streets where filled with cop cars.

"Yeah, we're handling it, Sarge. It was Bradford/Chen." A supervisor radioed in.   "Man. That's a lot of cops for a fender bender." I told him.   "Officer-involved accidents are very serious." He told me. He looked disappointed. I felt it too if I hadn't pointed out the skateboarder he never would have looked away from the road.

"Someone's getting a day at the beach." The supervisor took Tim's ID and walked off.   "Day at the beach?"That sounds nice.   "Suspension without pay. One of the many possible discipline options. I could be demoted, kicked out of field training. No point in taking the sergeant's exam." Okay not fun... and damn. Oh my gosh!   "Tim what if they think I was the distraction and not in a work way." "Dash cam. Thank god I haven't been turning it off. You'll be okay. "You will too. I'm sure of it." I smile and nod.   I more Grey and Harper pulling in, "And things just keep getting better." Tim looked less than thrilled.   "You two okay?" Grey asks us.   "Yeah fine." He said reassuringly.   "Shops not." Harper pointed out, man she was enjoying this.   "What happened?" Grey asked looking between us. Tim recollects what happened to Grey and Harper. Harper tells him to get looked at clear up that he wasn't impaired and to cover himself.   "Follow our shop back to the garage. Transfer our gear to a new one, pick me up at the hospital." "Yeah I'll do that." I nod and do as he asks.

While following the car I just keep replaying the scene in my head. I would have seen the brake lights. Tim would have seen the brake lights. Driving and patrolling is second nature to him. I get out and look over the car once we arrive at the shop. "You got business here little lady?" The mechanic asks me. "My part... TO and I were the ones involved in this accident." I told him gesturing to the car.   "Oh right. The beach boy." I ignore that little comment but will remember to use it to pick on Tim. "He's screwed."   "Have you looked at the other car yet?" I need to know if the brake lights were working. He said he hasn't yet. "There's something I can't get out of my head. I-I don't remember seeing brake lights." I tell him. "Uh-huh." He doesn't seem to believe me. "I heard the rumor about you guys... I believe he was distracted by you and now your trying to save him. I'll look when I have time." "You've got time now. This is important. The commander is aware of our situation and doesn't seem to think it affects our jobs at all. Now, Officer Bradford is a 12-year veteran. He's been wounded five times in the line of duty. He deserves your respect, not whatever macho crap this is." I calm down and a much nicer. "Sir." He huffs at me and goes over the trunk, "oh, tail lights weren't on." HA I WAS RIGHT, IN YOUR FACE!! He explains to me how it was done on purpose. "Insurance scams. See it all the time. Get someone to rear-end you and collect the settlement. Maybe your T.O. isn't screwed after all. Yet." "What's that powder?" I ask after seeing some red dust on the trunk. "Ah. Looks like your victim's into all kinds of scams." "What do you mean?" "Powder's, uh, red phosphorous. You know, the stuff on the tip of matches?" "Why would they have that?" I was so confused. "Well, if they're not cooking meth, arsonists use it to set fires. Harder to trace than gasoline, and you can make a fuse with it." Woah... way to go Tim!!

I go get a new shop after loading out gear into it I head straight to the hospital to tell Tim the news. "Hey you switch out shops?" "Uh yeah, but there's something else. The car was rigged!!" "What?" He looked so confused. "The brake lights weren't connected. The accident wasn't your fault!!" "No wonder I reacted so slowly. The leads were purposefully disconnected?" He seemed as relieved as I felt. "Yeah. And there's more. Sarah had arson materials in the back of her car.

Clearly, she's a bit of a renaissance scam artist." I explained "Let's go talk to her. And Lucy. Thank you so much."   "No problem." I touch his arm. When we get in there she obviously denies it all but we didn't give up. Tim got her info from her chart to run a background check. I cuffed her to the bed so she couldn't escape in the mean time.   We get the guy who was Sarah's emergency contact and probably boyfriend in an interrogation room.   "I think you should interview him alone." "Why?" I ask him confused.   "Because he knows I'm the one that hit her. He doesn't know you were in the car with me. His guard won't be up." I felt nervous... and apparently he could tell, "hey you got this. I trained you right, it'll be just like me in there."

I do the interrogation and he denied everything. Ever driving the car, being the one to do it. And he just gets up and leaves. I follow quickly to see him bump into Tim.   "I know what's going on here. You're trying to intimidate me. But it's not gonna work. 'Cause I'm gonna get a lawyer, I'm gonna come back here, I'm gonna sue you and the entire department." He told him.   "Little advice – if you can only afford one retainer, I'd start with a criminal lawyer. You're gonna need that one first." Tim let him go past.   "Sorry I didn't get more out of him." I tell Tim feeling like I let him   "Don't be. The point was to wind him up. First thing he's gonna do is call Sarah and wind her up even more." "And then we see who breaks first."

I tell him.   "That's my girl." We high five and walk away. I head to the bathroom and then to get a bottle of water .

We head back to the hospital and sit down to talk with Sarah. She gave him up and confessed that he plans to murder someone's wife for a cut of the insurance money. It worked! Tim's a genius!

"Okay boot get ready your going to play the guys wife." "What. You want me to pose as someone whose going to be killed?" "You know I won't let that happen." He told me. "Trust me..."

I come out of the couples house this deal was made with dresses to somewhat look like her.   Garvey approaches me and I feel my heart beating too fast in my chest. But before he can shoot Tim and a huge chunk of LAPD surround him.

"Freeze! LAPD! Turn around! Drop your weapon! Drop your weapon! Keep your hands up! Sidestep to the right! Keep going! Get down on the ground! On your stomach! Hands out to the side! Now, don't move! Mike Garvey, you're under arrest for attempted murder." He stops and looks at me. "Nice wig, Boot." He winks at me. The arrest happens and the day ends Tim kept his job and gets his reward.   I of course am his date.

At the ceremony I am taking pictures of him and West with them while Lopez is looking over my shoulder telling them how to pose.   "You make that your home screen, you're gonna be running the Academy training course in a bomb disposal suit."   "I would never now it's my Lock Screen!" He looked at me like try me. "Listen, I wouldn't have gotten this stupid plaque if you didn't have my back today. So, you know, thanks." He told me. "For what doing my job?" "Do we really have to do Johns surprise can't we just slip out... back to my house. You can wear that wig." He wiggles his eyebrows at me. "Deal." I shake his hand and we make a run for it.

In the car, I try to call Lila and they answer, "oh my god, babygirl, hi, mommy misses you." "I miss you too mommy." "Daddy wants to know if I can come home early and come next weekend so he can work." "Does he? Well you tell daddy to call me tomorrow and we will figure it out okay." "Okay. I wuv you!" She says and blows me a kiss. I hang up and rest my head against the door feeling really sleepy. "Hey, what's wrong?" "Nothing. I'm just tired is all.." I yawn. "Well I guess we could save the wig for the morning." "Mmhmm." I say as I fall asleep.

Where's Lucy?

It's the following Saturday and Lila went to her dads since he missed last Saturday and Sunday... so I am out having a few drinks with Armstrong, West, and Nolan. Well everyone else is drinking I'm sipping on water. I told them I want to be sober incase Emmett calls about Lila. Tim is watching some football game tonight but it's good to be out with the boys again. Reminds me of the academy days before things with Emmett got bad.

"No, but seriously, what is it like dating a celebrity?" I ask West after coming home to find him with a celebrity on our couch!! "Awesome. Yeah, he can always get a reservation, and the parties are sick." He was so enthusiastic about it. Nolan mocks him by saying "reservations" in a dreamy tone causing us all to laugh. "Well, we're happy that you're happy." I told him. "Liar." "No I'm serious, me and Tim are happy and I want everyone to be this happy." I smile widely. "In my opinion, you and Tim have like the best cop relationship we've all seen it. You would never know your more than friends on duty unless we knew you. It's kind of freaky." "Well I want to be trained by the best." I said. "Even your dad wanted you with Tim, West." Armstrong reached for the pitcher but it was empty. I snatched it from him "Hey, no, no, no. Uh, I got it. I got it." I head for the bar elbow my way through the crowd, "Sorry. Excuse me." "Excuse me!" I try to flag down the bartender, "yeah okay." I'm annoyed now.

A man sitting at the bar says, "pace yourself it's a marathon, not a sprint." He tells me. I smiled and laugh a little. "Have you been waiting here long?" I ask him. "What month is it?" He asks. "Oh, maybe we should just hop the counter." I joke causing him to laugh. "Yeah, I'm not much of a hopper, but I am a rock star at creating diversion. How do you feel about small fires?" I laugh a little too hard. "Mm. Define "small."" I ask him. I shake his hand. "Caleb." "Lucy." "Nice to meet you. What brings you out on a Wednesday night?" He asks me. "Uh, I'm just...hanging out with some friends from work while my boyfriend is watching some game." "Wow he must trust you letting you come out with a group of guys to a bar." "Yeah you could say that he's a pretty good partner." I laugh inwardly at my corny cop joke. "Nice meeting you Lucy." He got up and left . That was weird... Finally the bartender fills the pitcher and I take it back to the table. "I'm gonna head home guys. Have a good night."

I can't shake that guy from my head... it's so weird.

The next morning I get in work with only minutes to spare and I run to the briefing room hair not even up yet. "At 0500 this morning, guards at Central California Women's Facility prepared prisoner 081316 for transport. Rosalind Dyer, the most rare of unicorns -- a female serial killer. For the last five years, she's been on death row, confined to an 11-by-8 cell. Today, she's coming to us. Now, before I get to assignment details, I want to defer to Assistant District Attorney Del Monte for background on Ms. Dyer. Sean?" As I'm listening to Grey I fasten my hair into a uniform regulated bun. He exchanges good mornings with us then gets down to business, "My name is Sean Del Monte. For those of you who are not familiar with this case, in 2015, Rosalind Dyer was convicted in the torture and mutilation killings of seven individuals." Armstrong cuts in, "but there is evidence that the body count is much higher." "In three of those seven murders, the bodies were never recovered, so now Dyer has agreed to show us the location of those three victims." Ridiculous... why should she be allowed to do that. "Excuse me sir, in exchange for what?" Tim asks the question probably on all our minds. "Well, her sentence will be commuted from death to life without parole." Like that's any better... I'd rather die than sit in a jail til I do die.

"Why the hell are we cutting her that break?" Tim asks... woah. A break? In my opinion death would have been the easy way out. She's nuts for not taking it. I look back at him confused. He must have missed the break. "Well, it's not for her. It's for the families of those victims. They've been waiting a long time for closure." Del Monte explained. "Yeah, what about the other families? The ones that we promised the death penalty? What do we tell them? 'Cause they're calling me." Armstrong seems to not be happy about this at all and I don't blame him. I remember this case. He was a lead detective on it. "Just tell them it's above your pay grade, Detective." "Why does she have to come here? Can't she just tell you where the bodies are?" Lopez asked another million dollar question. "She claims not to know their precise locations. Griffith Park is over 4,000 acres. Dyer says the only way she'll be able to identify the dig sites is by retracing her original footsteps." Del Mint explained... no I learned about this in school she's going to relive her kills. "Sounds like an excuse to get out in the sun, relive her kills." Harper read my mind. "Maybe, but she knows if she doesn't lead us to all three bodies that the deal is off, so..." Del Monte motions for Grey to take back over. "Okay, let's get down to it. First, the station needs to be locked down for her arrival. Processing is officially closed for business. All suspects in our holding cells will be shipped to the Twin Towers."

Nolan, West and I were sent down to Bill Pen to get the prisoners ready for transportation. "This is so surreal. An honest-to-God serial killer?" Nolan seems intrigued to say the least and I don't blame him. They truly are interesting to learn about. "The psychology is pretty fascinating -- well, biology, really. Brain-scan research shows clear differences in the amygdala and the supramarginal gyrus of a signature killer." "English?" West asks. "They lack the ability to feel empathy. There's also data that suggests some psychopaths could have a decreased sense of smell." I told them. They begin talking to the criminal and my mind goes to back to that face from the bar last night... it looked so familiar.

I soon met up with Tim in the hallway and we were walking to the sally port. "I was in college when they found the first victims. It was all anyone talked about -- that and "How could a woman be so barbaric?" I told Tim as we walked down the hall to get ready for the transport.

"I worked one of the scenes. Fourth victim -- Lisa Cruz. Homicide detectives warned me not to look at the body. Should've listened." He told me back. "Oh my god.." The creepy guy from the bar. Maybe Tim will scare him off. "Lucy." "Uh. Hey." I say and wave small. "You left last night before I could give you my number." He told me and tried to hand me a piece of paper but Tim took it. "I told you, I have a boyfriend." I looked at him and then to Tim whose jaw was tight as can be. "Officer Bradford, you got a last name there Caleb?" He asked. "Uh, yes sir. Wright, with a "w"." "Well I believe Officer Chen here said she had a boyfriend. So scram." Caleb walked away pretty quick. "Really Lucy." Tim stalked off.

Once Rosalind was ready for transport they radioed all units to there positions. Tim and I would be following in our shop to provide an escort. Emmett messaged me "we need to talk." I keep thinking of that Caleb so damn familiar... I feel like it has... Tim cut me off mid thought making me lose my train of thought.   "Get your head in the game. Today's the most dangerous day you've ever spent on the job." He told me. "If anything happens to you, it's going to hurt a lot of people." I shove my phone in my uniform pocket and get my head in the game. "I just need to know.... Are you mad at me? I swear I told that guy I had a boyfriend last. I even left early because he creeped me out." "No Lucy. I was just..." he pauses, "taken back." "Okay."

We pull up to a stop behind the van. They let her out keeping her hands cuffed at her waist. She didn't look a serial killer at all. In fact she looked gorgeous.   "How did you carry a body all the way up here?" Nolan asks , him and his questions. Is he ever going to learn?   "Oh, he was still alive at this point. Thought we were going on a picnic. There was a moment, as we got deeper in the woods, when he showed just a sliver of fear, but then he remembered he was a man and didn't have to worry about things like that."   She points out the body is up the way a little Tim and I brought up the rear ...   "Okay so you met the monsters is she less scary in the light of day?" He asks me. "Not really, think she'll try to escape?" I ask him. I doubted it to be honest . "I hope so it would be suicide. She wouldn't make it more than 10 feet."   "She's smart. I mean, to have killed for that long, undetected. Maybe there's a play we're not seeing." I start to feel queasy. "Yeah, to jerk around the police, feel like she's in control again -- that's her play." I stopped dead in my tracks and emptied the contents on my stomach . "Boot, your gonna have to learn to work in the heat or figure out what's wrong with you." He hands me a bottle of water. "Sorry, sir." It's killing me to not tell him... I just can't do it... I can't be the pregnant rookie. We catch up when soon we hear shooting. Tim sees Del Monte go down and tells me to flank him. He's complaining he can't see. But shots are still flying .

We soon spot the culprit, one man with a rifle. "Drop the gun! Drop the gun! Put it down on the ground now! Hands up in the air! Hands behind your head! Interlock your fingers! Who else is with you?" Tim says cuffing him and disarming in. "Nobody." "Are you trying to free Rosalind?" I ask him... what is this guy doing? "Free her? I'm trying to kill her. She murdered my wife." My heart immediately aches for him... I couldn't imagine. Being subjected to that pain.

Grey gets the run down of the excitement from Armstrong. Tim and I walk the shooter down the hill. By the time we do the trade off a body is being hauled down the hill. Followed by another? Man that was quick. I soon find out that they discovered a new body and now we are on our way to the morgue. "This is your first decomp, right?" Asks me. "Uh, yeah." I nod feeling a little nervous actually. "Hope you emptied your stomach well out there." The elevator doors open to show a man standing outside them that Tim greets as, "Solomon." "Hey, Bradford. This your mess?" He asks "Yeah for now," he looks at me and asks, "you good." "Yeah." I barely whisper but he heard. His face relaxed instantly.

While looking at the body we discovered the new one was indeed not Rosalind. The new killer tattooed DOD on the body and the body was ruled death by asphyxiation but not a quick way... the lady screamed her self to death, trying to claw her way out of something metal. It was nerve racking and scary to be honest. It will have been 6 months ago, tomorrow since the death... We leave the morgue to meet up with Armstrong at the prison. "Lucy are you sure your okay. Your pale, your eyes are sunk and you've been throwing up a lot lately." "Tim I'm fine." Saved by a short ride. "This conversation isn't over." He tells me as we get out . "I don't know what you think you're gonna find. We've tossed Rosalind's cell top to bottom, every item in there." Hernandez the guard told us. "Hey, you never know. Sometimes a fresh set of eyes can help." We are in her cell tossing the few items she has. Looking over the walls, flipping mattresses, blankets, even checking the toilet. "This is a dead end." Tim shook his head and exhaled defeated... "Yeah," Armstrong steps back and looks around again... a look of realization crosses his face, "Where are the books?" "What?" I ask. "The books. Rosalind was a voracious reader. There would be books." Armstrong asked the guard. "She sent them back to the library a couple days ago." He answer him. "Right before she came to us." I mentioned... no way she was using books to communicate. "She knew we'd search her things. I need to see every book she checked out in the last... six months." Going through all the books she's had... I find a code. It was another clue. Armstrong starts flipping through. Clue to clue to clue. It spelt out "Bryan Coleman". We then look up the name and get an address but all it does is lead us to a message for Armstrong. Pictures of his deceased wife all over. And the words "you failed her" written in red ink.

When we arrived back at the station we met back in the briefing room. I felt my phone go off but I ignored it for now... John and Harper saved a woman whose death was next. But Bryan Coleman escaped... but his face is everywhere. He will be caught. Grey is sending us all home for the night. Once the meeting is over, I check my phone. "Meet me tonight at Las Torres. 1 hour, it's about Lila -Emmett."

"Hey, want to come over have a few drinks? After a day like to day it's good to blow off steam. Give your brain a different focus." Tim asked. "Emmett needs to talk. I can come over after." I tell him. "Shouldn't I go, incase he tries something?" Tim asks. "No I need to build confidence and plus it's in a public place. I'll see you in about 2 hours." I kiss his cheek and head to shower and get dressed.

I then make the drive to Las Torres and go in I find Emmett talking to Caleb? I knew he looked familiar. "So, you did know me last night." I raise an eyebrow and sit down. "Actually no, you know my buddy Emmett?" "You could say that." "Well nice seeing you Emmett I should get going." "I got you a glass of water." He slides it to me. "Cut the crap. What do you want." I ask him. "I want to have Lila when I can actually see her and not send her to my moms to go to work." "The courts made up the schedule not me. It works to where your off 2 of the 3 days. Unless your schedule changed." I tell him. Taking a few gulps of my water. "I work when I have her too most days." "Yeah 12s not 24s." "Well we knew having her we would have jobs that we worked long hours. Now if you don't mind I had a long day." I start walking to the car. I feel weird, weak, wobbly. "Well there. What do we have here." I hear from behind me and I see a blurry Emmett. I turn around but lose my footing a little and catch myself. "Worked like a charm Em, good job." It was Caleb and Emmett... they did this to me. "Drugged me." I whisper before I pass out.

How to Save Lucy

Tim's POV   It's been 3 hours and Lucy's still not here. Not picking up for me when I call. I'm getting nervous. Something just isn't sitting right.   Maybe she stood me up? No she wouldn't do that...   I grab my phone and call Jackson. "West, is Lucy there?"   "No she texted me about 2 hours ago. Said she was meeting with Emmett at Las Torres then going to your house. Told me not to wait up."   "Thanks she must still be there." I chug the last of my beer. I begin pacing back and forth, go to the fridge and grab a beer. Somethings not right. One more hour. I give her one more hour and I'll go look.

Lucy's POV I wake up and don't recognize my surrounding. My arms and legs feel paralyzed. I can't move. I soon realize I'm tied down. And someone's doing something really annoying on my ribs.   I life my head up and see Caleb from the bar tattooing DOD 12919 on my torso.   "Mm," I moan a little unable to find words.   "Thanks for helping me get rid of her."

I hear a voice I recognize and can't stand say exactly who it is. "No problem her little friend messed with my last victim." "Is that all you need from me?" I finally put a face to the voice. Emmett. The same man who tortured me for years. "Yeah, get out of here, we are going to have tons of fun. I'll meet you later when the jobs done." He grins evilly and I hear a door close and shut. "You know what that is?" He looks at me and to the tattoo, I nod. "Tell me" he demands. "Day of death."

Tim's POV "I'm telling you something is not right. She's not answering me." I tell Grey standing outside his office. "Sergeant!" Harper yelled followed by Nolan and West. "Tell him." She said. "Lucy didn't come home last night. She's not responding to our texts or calls." "See I told you." I tell Grey. "She went to meet Emmett at Las Torres about Lila and never came over or went home." If something happens to her I'll never forgive myself. I should have went . Something is not right... this Caleb guy showing up around her. Emmett as far as I know texted her right after Nolan saved the DOD girl, Nora I think was her name. "I'll go check her last phone ping and Emmett's." Harper said and walked off. "Run the name Caleb Wright as well." I yell after her. "Creepy stalker guy for the bar?" West asks and I nod my head. I need to hold it together. This is the ultimate test of if we can separate our relationship and work relationship, all eyes are going to be on me. Me spinning out will not help find her. We all enter the briefing room. "Everyone, listen up! Officer Lucy Chen has not been seen for approximately 13 hours. Last known to be meeting her Ex Emmett Lang at Las Torres known for abusing her. Given the circumstance, we cannot rule out abduction. So stop whatever you're doing. I want everyone on this until she's located. Notify S. O., see if they can shag calls for service." I felt everyone's eyes on me as I tried to hold it together. "What are you all staring at, find her!" I snap at them. "Phone company says GPS is disabled. Last tower ping was on Sixth and LaBrea at 9:07 last night. Same with Emmett." Harper came in with some kind of information. "That's close to where she met Emmett." "Control I need a shop to swing by Las Torres looking for an missing officer Lucy Chen." Grey calls out on the radio. I stand up and start pacing. He order Nolan to go talk to the victim he saved for any kind of information. I pull out my phone and dial Lopez's number, "hey, Lucy's been taken I need you." "Of course. What can I do?" "Go to Emmett's he was with her last night at Las Torres claimed to need to talk about Lila. It's either him or Caleb some creep that stalked her at the bar the night before." "I'll call you when I know something." She said and I hung up. "Sarg, give me something to do. I need to feel like I'm doing something." "Follow me." I follow him out to Armstrong's office. "Caleb Wright does not exist." He told us. "That's the name the guy gave us. Caleb Wright with a "w"." "Well that doesn't exist just like Bryan Coleman." "Exactly. He stole his life to gain access to the old zoo. Used its isolation to kill his victims."

Armstrong tells me.   "But with that place burned, he's gonna need new killing ground." I finish for him... the thought is sickening.   "My guess is he already has one, and that's where Lucy is right now." Armstrong tells me. I breath out heavily to hold my composure... but it's nearly impossible. The love of my life is out there missing.   "Let's go." I bark out .

Lucy's POV I wake up again to find myself restrained to a chair... I feel cramps in my stomach, either from hunger or just the anxiety of not knowing what's going to happen.   When Caleb enters eating some food, "Oh, hey. You're up. I'd offer you some, but it's better if your stomach's empty, you know, later. All the screaming tends to make you..." and he imitates gagging noises.   "Can-can I at least have some water..." I ask . I remember with Lila I would drink water to soothe my cramps. "Oh, of course. I'm not a monster." He gives me a few sips and immediately takes it back. "Dont be greedy."   "So is this why you talked to me at the bar? To get information to kidnap me?" I asked.   "No that was just luck. Your ex Emmett called and asked me to do him a favor after your buddy freed my last victim. I didn't know it was you, until you showed up last night. I ran into you scoping out Armstrong for Rosalind you were going to be my next victim 6 months from now... anyway, I don't know what she sees in him, Armstrong. PBut hey, who am I too judge. We all have our fetishes." I felt sick.   "I'm... I'm pregnant and I feel like I'm going to throw up." He brings a bucket over and let's me throw up in it.   "Woah, what to the pretty cop?" I nod. "Well we better get to it... I have a lot to do before I put you in the ground," he laughs . "Wait wait wait, why the tattoo? Is it some display of ownership? The ultimate control over another person, deciding when they die?" "No. It's not for me, silly. It's for you. To force you to face the truth of your death. It's the gift of something we rarely get in life. Clarity." If I wasn't so close to death I'd be thrilled to be picking the mind of a serial killer... but as a victim it's not as much fun. "Did Rosalind teach you that?" I ask him. "No! That's mine." I hit a nerve... time to play on it. "I just thought Rosalind is your mentor, so–" "No no no, it's not like that, we're equals." He defends himself. "Does she know that?" He glares at me then back hands me. "You're good, Officer Chen. I'm gonna enjoy this. More than I thought I would." He tells me.

Tim's POV My phone rang revealing Lopez's name, "well?" "He was just pulling in at his house. Said he was picking up Lila." "And last night?" "He claims they met they talked and she left. Some blonde guy followed her outside. He seemed truthful about the blonde. But when he said he left he started sweating. I'm bringing him in. I have Wesley with me. He'll look after Lila." "Caleb... Caleb is blonde!" "Okay keep me updated." I shove my phone in my pocket and turnt to Grey. "It's Caleb, Bryan or whoever the hell the creep is. Emmett is with Lopez on the way to the station." I tell Grey. "He knows more... Lopez feels it. I do too."

Lucy's POV.   I keep wiggling and fighting to get out of my restraints finally I break free.   "Okay we're ready to go." He comes near me and I take the chance and I punch Caleb and run out of the house screaming but I trip on a trip wire. I stand up and look around... my hands and knees sting. I force myself to stand up and there's nothing for miles no sign of habitation, cars nothing. Caleb runs out after me. I start to run but my ankle hurts and he's faster than me.   We start to struggle, me on top at first and then he reaches up and knees me in the stomach ... causing me to scream out in pain and land on the ground. Then he kicks me in the head and I see nothing but darkness.

Tim's POV   "Thanks for coming in." I tell Lopez as she escorts Emmett to a interrogation room.   "Of course, Grey's got you on tip lines?" She asked .   "Says I'm too close to this." He's not wrong but, I am probably the best option for her to be found. We have a pull that I can't describe.   "Tiiim." Lila reaches for me from Wesley's arms and she looks just like her mother, it hurts to look at her but I feel whole holding her in my arms.   "Hey my sweet girl." I tickle her belly a little. "Where's mommy?" That about breaks my heart.   "Mommy's out working." I tell her.   "Why you here. You keep mommy safe." I frown at her a little, I couldn't keep her safe this time. "How about you hang out with my friend Wesley while I go and keep mommy safe, okay?" I hand her to Wesley and stalk to the locker room. I slam a locker shut and punch it. I let the tears out. I can't lose her. I can't let her daughter lose her. I storm out of the locker rooms and down the hall into the interrogation room Emmett is in. "Where is she." I get in his face. "I don't know. Like I told your friend. We talked she left and a blonde followed her out back. She seems to have a thing for them now." "Tim, back off. This isn't helping her." Lopez was in the room pulling me back. "Why do you look so smug. Your kids mother is out there probably with a serial killer and your smiling and making digs at her." Lopez slams her hands down. I walk out only to move to an observation room. "I told her this job was going to hurt Lila more than anything. That she can't be both." "Well news flash. She kicks ass at both and your wrong." She leaves the room to join me in the observation room. "I'm going to beat it out of him. I know he knows." I tell her. "Yeah me too. But all that's going to do is get you in trouble and off the case completely if not worse." Lopez reminds me. "Dammit! I punch the wall." "If someone who isnt me would see this. You and Lucy would separated as TO and Rookie you need to pull it together Tim. She needs you now and when she returns. We will find her." "I let her go alone. I felt something that told me to go and I ignored it okay. She told me she would be okay and I believed her. I should have insisted on going with that assholes track record with her." I let my confession out and I felt the weight lift from my shoulders. "Tim this isn't your fault. You couldn't have known." "But I should've. I'm a cop. I was standing this close to the guy. Okay? Right across from him, and I never saw him coming. And Emmett I should have never let her meet him. He's done nothing but hurt her... so many times even since I've been with her. And I do nothing Angela. I just let him. I'm as bad as him." I cried. I heard her lock the door. I let it out for a good 2-3 minutes. "Okay enough. Your done. Your going to pull it together. And your going to put all those feelings into finding Lucy. You hear me?" I nod. "When he wants to talk, let me know what he says."

Lucy's POV Caleb now has my arms zip tied together walking me to my impending death. I hurt my ankle when I fell and now have a limp. To make matters worse he's poking me with a knife. I try to walk faster but my ankle is killing me and the cramps in my stomach are almost unbearable. I let the sobs come out as we walk He pushed the knife a little harder, "ahhh, if I get a hold of that it's going straight into your brain." That's when I doubled over from the pain in my stomach and I felt my pants get wet. I looked and there was blood between my legs and a lot of it. "Oh how sad, good thing your going to die soon and not have to deal with the guilt." He pushed the tip into my back again. "I can't wait to stab that knife right in your face." I spit at him. The grief... I never even got to tell Tim I was having his baby. I was going to do it last night but somebody ruined my plan.

"Such bravado Still thinking there's an escape. You weren't conscious for your birth, but you will feel every second of your death." He told me . Where does he come up with this shit.   I felt the pain ripping through my stomach, my ankle, and my head but with each push of his damn knife I pushed on.   "That's some greeting card level villainy. Not that psychopaths are known for being original thinkers." I told him.   "I know what you're trying to do, but you're not gonna ruin this moment for me. Let's go." He said. I kept walking and sobbing as I walked. I lost my baby... I can't handle this. The grief. The pain. To be honest. I just want him to end me.   I saw a barrel by a pre dug hole. I lifted an eyebrow at him.   "Aah! This is new. You suffocated the other two victims above ground before you buried them with Rosalind's kills." "Given the setbacks, I'm taking extra precautions. Climb in." I laughed at him a little. "I'm not getting in there."   "You know, they all say that. And then they all get in. You know why? Hope. Inside that barrel, there's still life."   He puts his knife away and grabs a gun instead and points it at me.   "Out here - Only death. And you and I both know, that despite the evidence literally tattooed on your side, you don't think you're dying today. So get in the barrel. Get down. " as I start to climb in the barrel I see my ring on my hand. I take it off and toss it without him noticing. I then sit in the barrel. "Look here." He takes a picture of me but I make the tears stop. "Any last words?" I know I have all of LAPD looking for me. I have more hope than any of the other girls did. I know Tim knew I was gone. West and Nolan. They know I would never miss work. "You'll be dead long before I am." I tell him with venom dripping from my words. He holds up the lid and has something taped on it, "so I can watch." He puts the lid on and I feel the barrel tip knowing I'm now in the hole.

Tims POV Armstrong got the name of the man who gets everything no in and out of the jail. That man is the man who helped Rosalind. He has to know something. Grey finally let me join the action after seeing my calm demeanor. "There he is, pull him over." West told me . I flipped on my lights and sirens. I turned off my body cam and the dash cam. I signaled for West to do the same. I walked up to his window, "problem officer?" I grabbed his head and smashed it into the steering wheel. Hard enough not to make horn go off but hard enough his sunglasses came off his face.   "You listen to me very carefully. Your name is Benjamin Lassie. You're a mid-level idiot, who controls every illicit item that enters the Central California Women's Facility. And today is your day of reckoning. Now, I am responsible for a life that is in jeopardy, and I will do whatever I have to to save her, do you understand? There's a man, who gives you items to smuggle onto death row for Rosalind Dyer. You are gonna give me that man." "Why would i do that?" He asks. Man I'm not in the mood for this shit right now. I need to find Lucy...   "Because if you don't I'll pull your insides out." I get awfully close to him.   "Jerry Havel." He said with a groan. "Call it in, West."

After calling it in we discover he is a guard for correctional facility. We gathered a SWAT team and we planned to over take Jerry Havel's house. Finally, we're getting closer to saving Lucy. "Go, go, go! Coming left. One down." Havel tried to run. I grabbed him and threw him down, "Get up! Where's Lucy." I screamed in his face. "Bedrooms clear." Another officer announced. "That's not Caleb. Damn it." I slammed my hand down on his coffee table. We established that Caleb stole his identity as well as Bryan Coleman's to get closer to Rosalind and to manipulate things to his need. "Is this connected to the officer that's missing?" Havel asked. "Yeah. And you were our last shot at saving her." I stalked off.

We head back to the station and keep searching and combing through any and all information.

There was a call in to go to a graveyard something about a cop in distress. I take the call because I just need to step away from it and it may be connected. West, Lopez, Grey, and I follow up on the lead. "Over here," Lopez yells. She shows us a photo of Lucy. Oh god she looks so scared and broken... I almost break, but if I do, I'll be pulled off the search. I hold it in. There will be time for feelings once Lucy is saved. On the back of the photo it read. "Now I have 2 cops." He took Armstrong too. Fuck. We could really use his skills and man does he have skills. He knows Rosalind better than all of us combined. I'm sitting in my shop thinking over all of this. Lopez and Grey head back to the station leaving me with West.

When I get a call a from Lopez. "Emmett finally broke. But before I go into detail you have to promise me you will not snap and you will stay level headed." "Tell me Lopez." I put it on speaker so West can listen. "He said, he was so mad about the custody agreement. That he called Caleb knowing about his sick tendencies and asked him to take care of her. Does he know where she is?" "No he said he saw her when she was first taken and when she woke up for a second but that Caleb planned to move her." "Dammit." I smacked my hand down on the steering wheel. "But Wesley has a theory... Caleb is obsessed with Rosalind right?" "Yes." "His theory is he's keeping Lucy somewhere related to Rosalind." "He's genius!" I felt hope again. But I fear this is the last hope. I drive back to the station, "how's Lila?" "She's good. Wesleys been coloring with her and took her to lunch. She's a great kid." "I know. Did anyone book Emmett?" "Yeah. A slew of things that should keep him locked up for a while." She told me. "Good. See you soon."

We get back and West takes a file he found where Caleb used Jerry's cards to rent a PO Box in Kerns. We then discover that Rosalind owns a farm in Kerns. FOUND HER!

Myself and Harper take a shop out, I refuse to wait any longer. The rest of them take a chopper to meet us out there so there is an above ground view.

Lucy's POV As I sit in the barrel I just go over every memory of Lila I can think of... Her birth. Her first birthday. When she said mama this first. Then I'm gained myself rocking her and what I imagine mine and Tim's kid would look like in a rocking chair looking out the window at a starry night sky as I'm rocking I sing to them.

"Stars shining bright above you Night breezes seem to whisper "I love you" Birds singing in the sycamore tree Dream a little dream of me Say "Nighty night" and kiss me Just hold me tight and tell me you'll miss me While I'm alone and blue as can be Dream a little dream of me Stars fading, but I linger on, dear Still craving your kiss I'm longing to linger till dawn, dear Just saying this Sweet dreams till sunbeams find you Sweet dreams that leave all worries behind you But in your dreams whatever..."

Harper and I finally arrive at the house. We drove lights and sirens the whole way there up a winding dirt road. "LAPD unit on site we cannot wait for SWAT. We are going in." I radio in. Harper loads a sniper rifle and goes around the back. As I go to the front. I breach the door, "LAPD, drop the gun." He has turned the gun from Armstrong to me. "Oh, the pretty boy... how'd I know you'd be the one to find me." He chuckles... "Where is she." I ask him no need for small talk, I have 1 thing on my mind... well 2. But finding Lucy is first. "Oh somewhere out there. I can't even remember, so good luck. Oh and my condolences... wether you find her or not you've lost your child." Child? "What do you mean." I ask... "Oh Lucy, she told me she was pregnant, probably thought I would let her go and feel bad. How stupid of her. Then stupid bitch tried to run. I kneed her in the stomach and sometime during her walk down death row she miscarried." That's when Harper pulled and shot him in the abdomen. "You guys take care of him . I'm going to find my girl." "Yeah. Go and Tim, I'm sorry." She said. I nodded and walked out the door. There is miles and miles of sand and dirt... oh Lucy where are you?

West walks up beside... "he wouldn't have buried her close to the house. Let's go." We start walking and my mind races as I scan every inch of dirt as we walk. For anything that looks out place. Lucy was pregnant... why didn't she tell me? How did I not see it? The constant throwing up. It's always been hot... it never affected her before. All the ice cream. The mood swings. And all the bathroom stops. Not drinking. How was I so blind... but now I'll never get to chance to know... Airship radioing in breaks my thoughts, "Airship to ground. Hate to say it, but there's a lot of possible sites visible from up here Mostly east and north." Fuck. Come on come one... where are you? "Let's split up. You go left, all right?" I keep walking a little ways when something shining on the ground catches my eye. I run over to it. It's Lucy's ring. I start moving sand and I feel the barrel. "I've got her! I've got her!! Right there." I yell and tons of officers meet me and start digging with shovels and there hands . Theres tons of chatter in the background but I just keep digging and the lid is soon visible. "Here. Come on! Here she is. Help me." We remove the lid. And there she is.

Unconscious covered in blood... but we found her. We pull her up. "Is she breathing?" Someone asks. No pulse. I immediately start CPR.   She starts gagging and coughing and crying all at once. I pull her into my arms and cry with her.. this is unbelievable. We saved Lucy. I found her. She's back to me. I can't believe it.

A Shell of Lucy Chen

Our reunion was soon broke up by her being pulled onto a stretcher. "She's hemorrhaging..." I hear someone say. "She was pregnant... but she lost the baby. I didn't know til Caleb told me." I say... and everyone's heads snap to me as I let out a pained sob. "Come on you can ride with her." They life flighted us to Shaw Memorial.

When we arrived at the hospital they separated us again. They took Lucy to a room to assess the physical damage and I sat helplessly in the waiting area alternating it with pacing back and forth. "Hey, how you doing?" Angela came and sat by me with Wesley. Who handed me a cup of coffee. "Wesley were is Lila?" I asked. "Nolan and West took her home. It's been a long day." "Thank you. For everything, both of you." I tell them. "Of course." "She was pregnant... with my kid." I choke out. "Was?" Lopez said. I looked at her and her eyes were full of sorrow. "Yeah... he told me. He kneed her in the stomach for trying to escape. I didn't even know." "This blood on me ... it's from her losing our baby." I stare down at my bloody uniform. She pulls me into a hug again and I just rest my head on her shoulder and cry. Lucy's saved. Im allowed to break down now.   "Here, I brought you clothes." She handed me a bag.   "Thanks." I take the bag and go change. I shove the dirty uniform back in the bag.

Soon after changing I heard my name, "Officer Bradford." "Dr. Sawyer. How is she?"   "She's sustained a good bit of injuries and she's going to have a long road of recovery mentally. But she's going to make it." I let out a deep breath and I smile, a small one but a smile none the less.   "Thank you."   "Come sit, let's talk." I nod.   "She has a sprained ankle with some torn ligaments, severe bruising to the abdomen. I was able to seal her head wound with a glue that will leave almost no scar. But she did lose a baby."   "I know... Ca— that asshole told me." "I'm guessing it was yours." I nodded at her.   "You know she's not going to come back from this easily. Losing a baby is one thing. But losing one because someone did it to you on purpose is different."   "I know. I'll be there for her." I tell her looking down at the ground."   "I know you will., once she's settled in a room I'll have someone come get you." She pats my shoulder and walks away.

Lucy's POV   Light the light... it's bright... I open my eyes and look around. I'm in a hospital bed. I open my eyes and look around. Theres Tim sitting in a chair reading something I can't make out.   "What are you reading." My voice sounds awful.

"Lucy, your awake." He gets up and moves near me pulling the chair with him. "You found me." I say with a small smile. He hands me some water and I chug it all almost instantly. "I did." He nods and runs his hand down my hair and kisses my head. "I was so scared." I tell him as I wrap my arms around him and let the tears come out. "I know... baby." After a few minutes of him holding me, he pulls away. "I hate to do this right now. But, I can't keep torturing myself..." he paused and looked in my eyes. "Why didn't you tell me?" I knew exactly what he meant. Of course he knew now... there was no missing the message of blood that covered my pants before I was buried. "I was going to tell you when I came over after meeting... him. I was waiting because I didn't want to be known as the pregnant Rookie." "Lucy, we could have kept it to ourselves. You need to keep me in the loop about stuff." He looked me in the eyes. "No more secrets." "I'm so sorry I couldn't protect your baby. I thought telling him would maybe make him let me go... but I was wrong. I was so wrong." I shook my head and tried to get the thoughts out of my head. "Lucy, don't. Don't you dare feel guilty this is NOT your fault." I went limp in his arms and he held me up as I mourned the lost of my child.

"Glad to see your awake." Dr. Sawyer came in the room and gave me a weak smiles "There's a few guests out there for you. Do you want me to ask them to come back?" "Is Lila out there?" I need to hold my baby. "Yes she is. Bring Lila in please." Dr. Sawyer said out the door. Soon Nolan and West walked in.

West holding Lila and Nolan a giant pink teddy bear. Lila squirmed to get down and when she was she ran to me. Tim helped her up on the bed and sat down at my feet. I held on to her. "So what has my girl been up to?" I touched her nose and smiled the most genuine smile anyone will get out of me for a while. Well actually only Lila will get these smiles. I am beyond broken but she is my reason to fight. "Hmmm coloring, eating. Your friends fed me a lot of food mommy." We all laugh at her. "I didn't know what else to do." West shrugged. "Thank you guys."

"Can you show Lila to the cafeteria while I speak to Officer Chen and Bradford please?" Sawyer asked Nolan. "Sure." "Ugh more food. Im going to need bigger clothes." Lila threw her hands up and walked out holding Nolan's hand.

"Lucy, I'm sorry to tell you but you suffered a miscarriage. Your abdomen is severely bruised as well as a sprained ankle. And some scraps and bruises." I nodded. "I know... He he... kneed me when I tried to escape. I did this." I sobbed again. For the loss of my baby. Because I almost died. Because I was buried alive. "Lucy hey hey, you didn't do this. You lack of oxygen would have been enough to do it... it would have happened either way. So don't you for a second think this is your fault." Dr. Sawyer was holding my hands. "You are a fighter. You fought til you couldn't anymore. You survived." She let go of my hand and stepped back. "I am very sorry for your loss, both of you." "Thank you." Tim said with a curt nod. "When can I go home?" I asked her. "Tomorrow probably. We need to observe you and make sure you won't need another blood transfusion and you definitely need rehydrated with IV fluid." "Thank you." I tell her.

West comes back in with the bear. "Nolan said this is the biggest he can find." "I'm going to need another apartment." I tell them with a laugh. "Listen he is not getting my room, uh Uh. Nope." West jokes. I smile a little. "Oh, thank you! Well, he is a she, and she is going to sleep in my bed, since I am clearly, never going anywhere alone again." I state firmly. "Definitely not." Tim says grabbing my hand. I smile weakly at him. I shot up from my bed. "EMMETT! Did anyone get him? He was apart of this... he wanted me taken care of." I say quietly at the end. "Yes after hours of sitting in a interrogation room he cracked and gave himself up." "Are you hungry?" Tim asks. "Yeah, you know what I could really go for?" I ask. "A veggie burger and fries with extra pickles?" He asks. "You know me so well." He pulls out a bag. And I get to eatting. Lila came back to visit til they asked her to leave.

The next day I was discharged and Tim hasn't left my side. The nightmares when I sleep are unbearable even with the medication they gave me to help. He was driving me home where Lila is with the sitter since everyone else is at work. Given that I'm Tim's rookie they gave him some time off as well. "Why don't you come stay with me for a couple weeks?" Tim asked.   "I... I don't know. I just want to shower and change.." "Sure. Of course." He helps me up to my apartment. My ankle was in a splint and I had crutches from the trip wire.   I get in the door and Lila comes running up to me. "Hey baby." Tim sees the sitter out for me. But I saw her... staring with eyes that said she felt sorry for me. I can't face it. "Mommy's going to take a shower okay. Tim's going to sit with you." She nods. I get up and go in the bathroom. I slowly undress. I look at my body. A cut on my face. Two small cuts on my back. A bruised abdomen. I run my hand over it imaging myself with a small baby bump. And then my eyes catch it the DOD tattoo on my ribs... I forgot about thats I let out scream and Tim is at the door trying to get in. "Lucy are you okay?" "Uh... y-yeah. Sorry I was just spooked." I say. "Do you need me to come in and sit while you shower? I will." "N-no. I-I'll be out soon." I say with a shaky voice. Running my fingers over the tattoo. I get in the shower it's a tall stand up one and I sit down on the floor.   Suddenly I'm back in the barrel. I feel my heart beating fast. I feel trapped. I start pounding on the door.   "Let me out! Let me out!! Noooo." I'm screaming pounding with both my fists.   "Lucy!" Tim grabs me and pulls me out he puts a towel on me and holds me.   "I was there. I was sitting in the barrel waiting to die." I cry. "It's okay. It's okay." He runs his hands down my hair. "Here put this on." He helps me into my robe. His eyes stop on my ribs. "Lucy."   "I know..." I shove my robe closed and walk away. I go in my room and close the door and sink into the bed. Tim soon follows me. "Lilas taking a nap." "Okay." "I need to shower but I can't here. It feels like the barrel it's so small..." I tell him as tears prickle my eyes. "I'm sorry... I'm sorry I didn't tell you I was pregnant. I'm sorry that Ca— he was the one." "I wish I had known but that changes nothing Lucy." He sits down beside me and holds my hands in his. "We will get married someday and we will have all the babies you want, okay?" He then kisses me. I blink away the tears and kiss him back. "I went almost 24 hours thinking I had lost you, and now I have you back and I am NEVER letting you go again."

2 days later I'm sitting at Tim's at his breakfast bar picking at food. And I pick up my plate and throw it away. Lila is still at Emmett's mom. I'm still screaming at night and barely sleeping. Tim is ever faithful sitting by my side and holding my hand through it all. I decided after my mental break down in my shower to have Mrs. Lang take Lila til I'm better. She was more than willing and apologized profusely. But it was like after getting in that shower I was stripped of all the willpower I had to keep on fighting. I became a shell of Lucy Chen.

I got up and went to the bathroom locking the door. I undressed and looked in the mirror. The letters and numbers etched into my skin staring at me. "TIM!!" I screamed. Only seconds later he's knocking on the door. "Go get me cover up." "What?" "Go get me cover up. Please." "O-okay."

Tim's POV Lucy thinks I don't notice but I do. She's barely slept or ate in 2 days. Her already small figure even smaller. I'm scared to even leave her alone. What if she does something? What if she can't take the pain anymore? What if she ends her own life... she's refusing to go to the therapist the precinct wants her to see to return to active duty. I only have 2 weeks off with her then I have to return to active duty and if she goes on like this I doubt I'll be able to leave her.   "TIM!!" I hear her scream from the bathroom I was only sitting on the bed because I didn't want to go too far away. I knock on the door. "Go get me cover up." She says through the door. "What?"What cover up for, wh—- oh! "Go get me cover up!" "O-okay." I grab my car keys and drive down to the drug store. I grab her cover up that looks like it'll cover the black ink up. Then I see some flowers and grab those. I head back to the house and in to my room where I still hear the shower running. I also hear Lucy's sobs. I step in the hallway and grab her phone. Unlocking it I call Emmett's mom. "Mrs. Lang, Officer Bradford. I think you should bring Lila over. I'll be here the whole time and I really think it could break Lucy out of this trans shes in."   "Do you think that's a good idea?" "I really do. She was laughing and eating when Lila was with us. And now she's just this zombie." "Okay just send me your address. We will be there in the morning."   "Thank you." I hang up the phone and go to the bathroom again.   "Can I come in?" I open the door a crack and see her through the curtain. She's scrubbing vigorously at her torso. Her skin is red and raw. "Lucy. Stop, please." I grab her hand. She just stares. "Lucy, please. I need you back. I lost something too, okay. I lost my child, I lost my partner, and I lost you. Please come back. I can get you back." I stare into her eyes. "I'm sorry." She hugs me getting my clothes soaking wet, but I don't care. "Come here." I help her out. I grab a towel and pat her dry. Then I grab the bag of cover up and begin applying it to the tattoo and covering her in her robe. She walks to the bedroom and climbs in bed. I strip down to boxers and climb in beside her.

Lucy's POV   I lay in bed with my eyes clothes but I don't sleep. I can't sleep. The nightmares haunt me... I sometimes dream of us as a family of 4 while it's not a scary dream. It kills me. I hear Tim snoring and I continue to just lay there. I won't let dreams take me over. I can't. I don't know how I'm going to recover from this. It's not that I don't want to talk, eat or sleep. I physically can't. All I think about is showering to wash away all of the pain. So I just laid in bed and went over the criminal codes in my head all night. Until Tim's alarm went off. "Morning Lucy. You didn't have nightmares last night that's good." "Yes so good." I force myself to say for Tim. I grab clothes and go to the bathroom. I put on shorts and t shirt after covering the tattoo up again. Tim was outside the door already dressed. He never goes father than the room beside me and truthfully I'm thankful for it. I see flowers on the counter and I smile. He watches me take them and find a vase to put them in.   "I have a surprise for you." He says. I look at him. "Lilas coming over. She misses her mom." I stop and look at him with evil eyes. "Lucy I know your hurting but shutting Lila out isn't going to help." "I'm not shutting her out." I snap. "I miss her too. But she shouldn't see me like this." "Lucy at the hospital when she was with you. You were eating, talking, JOKING!" "It was an adrenaline rush. Look it up." I stomp off. I don't want Lila to see me like this. Bruised, broken, and hurt a zombie in the shell of Lucy Chen.

Rose

I sit at the breakfast bar at Tim's again and I feel my self dozing off. I see flashes. Caleb's face, Emmett's face, me in the barrel, the blood between my legs. Flashes in and out of my head every time I start to fall asleep and I snap my eyes back open. "Come on in. She's in the kitchen Lila." "Mommmyyy." Lila came running in the kitchen and jumped in my arms. "I miss you." I hold her in my arms and I breath in her scent, berries and vanilla. "Mommy can we go home?" "Not right now baby. Your going to stay with grandma for just a few more days, okay?" "But can we play for a few first." "Why don't you ask Tim for some crayons and paper." Before she even asked he was at the table with both things. I start to scribble Lilas name and draw little stars and hearts. "I'll be right in the living room if you need me." Tim says sitting a cup of coffee in front of me which I down eagerly. "Look mommy." She had a picture of me smiling and her holding my hand. I smiled a little at it. An hour passed by with Lila coloring me and smiling at her pictures and the occasional that's nice baby. "Can you make me pancakes?" She asked. "Grandma said I could have breakfast with you."

Tim's POV I handed Lucy some coffee and went in my living room where I sat down across from Mrs. Lang. "Your right she is a zombie." She told me.   "This is the most she's talked since Lila came to stay with you. I don't know what to do." I sigh and take a drink of coffee. "She didn't sleep last night. She doesn't know I know. But I do."   "Just give her some times. She's been through a lot, she'll bounce back. I've seen that girl overcome a lot. I never approved of how Emmett treated her. I'm actually glad he's behind bars. Not tainting Lila, not hurting Lucy. She's a good woman Tim." She shakes her head in disgust. "Is she going to speak to someone?"

"The departments willing to pay for therapy. She has an appointment tomorrow actually. I made it for her. She doesn't know yet. She missed her appointment yesterday. She refused to leave the bed." I recalled trying to get Lucy to get out of bed and she wouldn't move. She just laid there staring at the wall holding her stomach. The memory alone hurt my heart. I hate seeing her like this.

"Can you make me pancakes?" I heard Lila ask Lucy. I stood up and peeked in. Lucy got up and started looking in the cupboards. I smiled at her she moved for Lila. "Grandma said I can have breakfast with you."   "Yes sweetie." She began pouring the mix in a bowl and I stepped back. "I knew this would help." I look at Mrs. Lang who has a knowing smile on her face. "Im so sorry for what my son did to you guys. How are you holding up?" The older lady asked me. "I don't know. I haven't had time to deal. I've been taking care of Lucy." "Don't forget to take care of yourself too. Let's go check on them." She was right, besides being angry or sad for Lucy I haven't thought of how I feel. I know I'm relieved she's okay. I know I went through hell but, I didn't go through nearly anything as bad as Lucy. It doesn't seem fair to her.

Lucy's POV Im making Lila pancakes but I'm so tired. So so tired... I just want to go to sleep. The coffee did nothing. Tim and Mrs. Lang then walk in and sit down. I walk over to Lila and kiss her forehead, "Mommy loves you sweetie but I need to go lay down okay. Tim will make you pancakes before Grandma takes you back to her house. Mommy's boo-boos hurt." I look at Tim who frowns. "I wuv you mommy." I walk through the bedroom and to the bed. I lay down in the covers and soon a nightmare filled sleep takes over.

I'm back in the barrel and Tim pulls me out. I open my eyes and look at him. I notice movement from behind him. I look up and see Caleb. "TIM!" I yell. But Caleb drives his knife right through Tim's chest. "Gotcha!" He then shoves me back in and closes the lid again laughing.

"Lucy. Lucy!" I awake to Tim shaking me. "Lucy you need to talk to someone. This isn't normal! You don't eat, you don't sleep without being terrorized. You were yelling my name this time. You never do that. Talk to me what we're you dreaming about." He held my face in his hands.

"He got you. You saved me and he killed you and shoved me back in the barrel." I felt the tears running down my face. "I'm okay. I'm right here. I promise." He pulls me in and runs his hands through my hair again.

The next day "Lucy Chen. We are going to this appointment. I will carry you there over my shoulder in just that T-Shirt I don't care." Tim is currently trying to get me to go to a therapist. It's not that I don't want too at all. I'm not ready. "Lucy please. I have to go back to work in 10 days and I can't leave you in this state. I can't and you know they won't give me more time off." I throw a pillow at him and get up. I get dressed and walk out to Tim's car with him on my tail. He drives me to a fancy looking office and I walk in. Tim's signs me in and sits beside me. He is tapping his foot impatiently and keeps looking at me. "Lucy Chen." Someone calls my name I stand up and look at Tim. "Do you want me to come?" He asks. I nod my head. We both get up and walk in and take a seat on the couch. "Hi Officer Chen my name is Dr. Swan. And I'm assuming your Officer Bradford, whose been making Lucy's appointments." "Yes ma'am." "Pleasure to meet you both. And Lucy, how are you feeling today?" I just looked at her. So cliche... doesn't she know what I've been through, how does she think I feel? "Lucy this isn't going to work if you don't talk." Tim tells me. "I know how this works. She's going to make notes and listen to me talk and it's going to get nowhere. Psych major remember. The only thing that will help is time."

"She speaks!" Tim tries to joke. I didn't find it funny. "So I take it Officer Chen hasn't been speaking?" Dr. Swan asks. "Barely. Mostly when her daughter is around. She's having her stay at her Grandmothers til she's better." Tim explained to the doctor. "Tim how does Lucy not talking make you feel?" The Dr asked Tim and I looked at him. "Helpless... I need to talk to her about this but I can't because she won't talk. I don't know what she's thinking. She just stares." I didn't know I made him feel that way. "I just want to help her. That is my number goal." "I feel like everything I have ever known is just gone. I feel unsafe. Violated. I have the day I was supposed to die etched into my fucking skin. I can't even shower in my own home without thinking I'm going to buried alive. It makes me sick." I tell them both. "I just feel like everything I ever knew or felt is gone. My confidence, my happiness. It's all gone." "And why do you feel your confidence is gone?" She make a note on her note pad. "I was kidnapped by a serial killer and my ex to be killed. Im a cop! How did I not see it?" I look at Tim whose face was distorted into a feeling I could not read. "I understand you both lost a child during all of this? Do you want to explain to me what happened Lucy?" I freeze this is the hardest part of it all. The part I struggle the most with... well this and the DOD tattoo forever embedded as a memory in my skin. "I... I got my arms free from the restraints. I punched him hard enough to k-knock him out. I took that chance t-to r-run." I pause and look at Tim who is staring at me. "He had a wire set up to trip me. It... it worked. When he came through he came after me. I realized there was no-where, there was nothing I could do but try to fight. He kneed me in the stomach. Hard enough to bruise it and cause me to lose the baby.." I stopped and wiped the tears from my face. "I walked for miles covered in my own blood. Well I guess the babies too. I sat in a barrel and just bled and cramped up I felt it all. It felt like I was in labor again. But there was no baby at the end to make me forget the pain." I sobbed. I looked at Tim who was sobbing as well. "One last question for today then I have an assignment for you." I looked at her and cocked my head to the side. "How can you take this experience and make yourself stronger?" I stopped and thought... I don't feel stronger at all. Tim was staring at me. I bit on my finger nail. "I don't think I can." I shook my head. "You will Lucy. You signed up to protect and serve your community am I correct?" I nodded at her. "You will find a way to channel all this anger and hurt into your work. Remember this question right here... when you have an answer you tell me. Okay?" "Can I ask Tim something with you here?" I ask. "Sure. Go ahead." "Do you resent me for not telling you I was pregnant? You never got to enjoy the idea of being a father. You don't even have time to grieve." I look at him and he looks utterly shocked. "I...I," he pauses I can tell he's thinking because his eyebrows are furrowed. I hold my breath waiting for the answer. "I wouldn't say I resent you. I'm just confused as to why you hid it from me. I understand why you didn't want the word to get out. We already are under a microscope because I'm your TO and we fell in love. But, I don't know why you didn't trust me to know."That wasn't as bad as I thought. I let my breath out. "I was waiting for the right moment. I know we had plenty of moments. But, I guess something in me was scared you would treat me different. Stop taking the dangerous calls at work or something like that. Scared you would unknowingly hurt our careers by trying to keep us safe." I confessed to him my thoughts. "Not that I did a good job of that." I mumble but I know they heard me. "So that assignment?" Tim asked rubbing his hands together. "Yes, I want you both to go shopping. Buy a baby outfit and say goodbye to the baby. Close that door. I know the pain won't go away, but closure will help." I look at her. "What if I'm not ready to let go?" I whisper. "You need to Lucy. Or you never will recover from this. It doesn't have to be today. But it should be soon." "Thank you Dr. we will do that." Tim shook her hand and then looked at me. I shook her hand as well. "I'm going to schedule another appointment before we leave." He said. I look at him and nod. We get in the car and I look at Tim. "I don't want to let go yet." I tell him. "You tell me when your ready." He takes my hand in his and kisses it. "Can we go to my apartment? I need some more clothes." I ask him. "Sure." He starts the car and heads to mine and

West's apartment. When we arrive there I grab a bag and some more clothes. When I walk out I see West and Bradford talking. "Hey Luce." He waves at me and I wave back. "How's work going?" I ask. "Eerily slow. We are missing you guys tho." He smiles. "Hopefully I'll be back soon." I tell him. "I'm just going to use the restroom and I'll be ready to go." I walk in the bathroom and look at the shower. I sit down and do my business staring at it. I pull my pants back up and I open the door to the shower. I step in it leaving the door open. Okay this isn't bad. I start to shut the door and I have a flashback of the lid closing on the barrel and I quickly step out of the shower. "Come on Lucy. Lila needs you to snap out of it. Los Angeles need you to snap out of it." I say I'm the mirror. "Ca— he is dead. Emmett is in jail. You are safe." I sigh and leave. I still feel empty and lost.   "Ready?" I nod at Tim and we go back to the car. "Do you want to go buy the outfit?" He asks, and I shake my head. "Dinner? I can get you a veggie burger and fries with extra pickle?" I shake my head again. "Don't go back in your shell. Please don't do that to me again." I just looked forward. I don't want to but I'm not ready yet... When we arrive back at Tim's I go and lock my self in the bathroom like I do once a day. I step out of my clothes , and into the scolding hot water. I close my eyes and lean on the wall. My hand lands on my stomach and I cry. I picture myself holding her and Tim holding me while Lila sits on the bed between my legs. I'm smiling brightly. Then my finger touches the raised skin of the tattoo. I grab the loofa and scrub at it till I can't stand it anymore. I get out and use cover up on the tattoo. "Tim," I step into the bedroom. "I'm ready." I grab clothes and get dressed. Tim takes me hand and we go to the car and he drives to Target. We walk slowly to the baby aisle. The tears threatening to spill over. "I always pictured we would a have a girl." "Okay, how about this?" He holds up a pink sleeper with white polka dots. "That's perfect Tim." I give a small smile to him. "Okay. Let's go." We go to the gift box aisle and I choose a small square white box with a gold bow and we then go and check out. "Where do you want to say goodbye?" He asked me. "I know where." We arrive back to the house. I hold onto the sleeper and cry for a second Tim wraps his arm around mine and I look at him. He has a few tears as well. I place the outfit in the small box and close the lid. "The spots ready." We walk out back and under the rose bush he had a little hole ready. I place the box in it and Tim covered it with the dirt. "Rose, that's what I'm going to call you when I can think of you. When I was going through literal hell, you were there with me. You pushed me to fight back. I just couldn't keep you safe and I am sorry. Part of me aches that I'll never get to hold you, see you take your first steps or say your first words. But, I'd like to believe your in a place where no harm comes to anyone. You'll never know pain. Your dad and I love you and I will see you some day and when I do I'll get to hold you and never let you go." I turned to Tim whose face is streaked with tears. "That was beautiful Lucy. Rose... I love you. I can't wait to meet you someday." He kissed my forehead. We just stood there and looked at her spot for what felt like eternity. "Come on, you should try to sleep." He tells me. I turn away but I take one last glance and give her a small smile. I lay down in bed and soon sleep overcomes me. That night I sleep, I still have a few bad dreams, but I am able to return to sleep after being awoken.

The Road to Recovery

Tim's POV It's officially been a week since Lucy was saved. 4 days since we said goodbye to Rose. And 7 days before I go back on duty. Lucy is eating very small meals, sleeping but waking to nightmares and most importantly she's talking. Not much and unless she needs to or is spoken to but enough to make me feel like we can get back to normal. Right now we are sitting at the therapist office Lucy had something to tell me she didn't want to alone. "I think I'm ready to go back to the apartment with Lila." I spit my beer out mid drink. "Um, are you sure?" I ask her. "Yes. You go back to work in a week. You need to get back to normal. I need to learn to live without you holding my hand." She says confidently. I am not ready for this... I love having her in my home. Even in her upset state she makes it feel brighter and warmer. "You and Lila are more than welcome to move in with me." I blurt it out not even thinking before I say it but it just feels so right. "Tim, we went through something very traumatic in the beginning of our relationship. We have advanced way to fast. I am super super greatful for you being there for me and I love you. But I need to learn who I am." "Dr. Swan, please tell Lucy she's overreacting. There's nothing wrong with moving a little fast. Sure if the whole abduction thing and losing a baby didn't happen I could see this being too fast. But I'm ready. I mean you still stand in the shower and try to scrub your skin off for an hour everyday. You go and sit by Rose every morning... how are you going to do that from the apartment? You can't even get in the shower there without freaking out." "Lucy, are you sure your ready to do this? I mean Tim's not wrong. With everything you've gone through there's nothing wrong with advancing your relationship a little." I smile in victory. "BUT," she looks at me and I snap back to my resting face. "Lucy your not wrong either. Wanting to find yourself on your own is perfectly fine too. You were in a toxic relationship for a very long time and then you went through a traumatic experience." "Tim I will think about your offer. But tonight can we stay at the apartment with Lila?" She asks. Okay I feel better knowing she will think about it. "Of course." I grab her head gently and kiss her on the temple. "So Lucy how have you been since we last spoke? You look much better than before." The Dr. asked. And it's true. Her face isn't as pale, the dark circles under her eyes are still there but not as evident. I did notice she lost some weight in just a week: "Better. We said goodbye to Rose. I've been sleeping a little better, I'm forcing myself to eat but I never feel hungry so it's kind of hard." She looks at me with a small smile and I see the determination in her eyes I've seen plenty of times before. I know in that moment I will have my Lucy back.

Lucy's POV   Later that night Tim and I walk into mine and West's apartment.   "I need to do something. If Lila gets dropped off just hang out with her a second." He turns his head at me and looks confused.

I walk to the bathroom. I turn on the water and get undressed. I step in and close my eyes. I peek one open and close the door. Images flash across my face. The lid closing on the barrel, me being jostled around as I am kicked in the hole. Me banging on the lid and lastly me singing. I feel the tears flowing but I just stand there.   I grab a rag and start washing myself and then my hair. I look down at the damn tattoo and start to scrub. I stop myself... no Lucy this will not control you.

I get out of the shower and get dressed.   I run out to the living room and Tim is on his toes, probably looking for what's wrong. I jump in his arms and wrap my legs around him.   "I did it." I kiss him deeply and smile. "You did it." He smiles and kisses me back.   "Mommy," Lila runs out of her room and flings herself in my arms and I hug her.   "Hi baby."   "We home," she clapped her hands.   "Yes baby." I smile and kiss her forehead.

Later that night I lay in bed. I asked Tim to sleep on the couch tonight. Trying to get as close to normal as possible.

But still not ready to be alone. I'm tossing and turning. I stare at the ceiling. "Ugh." I groan. A few moments later I hear a knock on my door. "Can't sleep?" Tim asks. "No." "Me either." I sit up and pat the bed. "You know; I don't think it would be a bad idea for you and Lila to move in. I think it would be nice..." He started running my shoulder. He kissed it. I turned my head and kissed him. I turned my whole body and deepened the kiss. I pushed him back on the bed. "Lucy," he grabbed my roaming hands, "are you sure?" I nodded my head at him, "yes."

The next morning I woke up tangled in Tim's arms. Lila was crawling in bed. "Morning, sweetie," I kissed her temple. "Morning ladies," Tim woke up and stretched. I could do this everyday for the rest of my life. Wake up in Tim's arms to Lila bouncing in with us. I'm going to do it, because Tim isn't Emmett. I don't need to prove myself to him that I'm strong on my own. He already knows that. But I'm better with him, he makes me strong. Emmett, he did everything to break me "Let's do it." Tim gave me a smile that could light up the universe.

By the end of the day almost all mine and Lilas stuff were moved into Tim's. I guess our home now. Tim was standing in the backyard drinking a beer. I walked up and wrapped my arms around him. "What cha thinking about?" "Where to put a play set for Lila." He said. "Tim really that is so sweet." I reached up on my tippy toes and kissed his cheek.

1 week later.   I'm sitting in Dr. Swans office. By myself this time. Tim is only in the waiting room, but he goes back to work tomorrow and I am feeling nervous about being alone so much.   "Well Lucy. How have you been?" "Good, I showered at the apartment, Lila and I have actually moved to in with Tim." I say with a small smile. "Oh? And how do you feel about it?" She asked.   "I feel safe. You know, with Emmett he would build me down. But Tim he builds me up. He's there for me but he lets me choose for myself. He gives me the chance to be confident and always builds me up. The feelings are so difficult to put into words." "I understand." She nodded her head at me.   "There's one thing I feel like i just can't get past... I still feel like I lost my ability to judge people." I shake my head... and take a deep breath, "like how could I miss that Emmett did this to me? I felt like that Caleb guy was off, but I couldn't figure it out." "Maybe you should confront Emmett? As a psych major I'm sure you are well aware that many people who experience the trauma you went through recover very well after getting closure with there attacker. In your case the main attacker is deceased but, the one who put you in the position is not." She closed her notebook. "And that is the end of our session. You get that closure and I'll clear you to return to work and cut our sessions down to Bi-Weekly unless you need me otherwise." "Thank you." I get up and walk out.   The next morning Tim's alarm awoke me at 5 am. I rolled over and shook him gently. "Time for work. I'll get some coffee going."

I swing my legs over the bed and grab my phone. Once I hear the shower running I call Mrs. Lang. "Well hello." She says in a chipper voice. That woman never did sleep. "Hey, I need a favor." I tell her. "Sure, what is dear?" "Can you watch Lila for a few hours today? I need to go do something." "Sure honey, I'll be right over." "We kind of live at Tim's now." She bid me goodbye and I hung up. I finished brewing the coffee and made us both a cup. I met Tim at his bedroom and handed him one. "Well, how you feeling?" I ask. "I should be asking you that. It's your first day on your own since..." he trailed off and crossed his arms. "Yeah. I think I'll be okay." I nod my head. "I expect to be riding with you soon, boot." "Yes sir." I smile and hand him his cup. Once he kissed me goodbye I ran to the bathroom and put on jeans and a tank top, topping the look off with some converses. When Mrs. Lang arrived I told her to make her som comfortable and that I should be home by lunch. She didn't ask questions and I was thankful. I soon arrived in front of the Cal Correctional Facility. I went in and signed in. They asked for ID and they ran a metal detector over me. Now here I am walking back to the man who broke me down and quite literally set me up for death. I was separated by the glass from him when he walked in. We both picked up the little phones. "What do you want?" He asked. "To know why. Why did you have so much anger for me that you set me up to have me killed." I ask him in disbelief. "Believe it or not I loved you Lucy. Then you became the exact opposite of what

I loved about you. Before you were a cop you were carefree and fun. Then you started the academy and you became this uptight person. You were more cocky then confident." "You sure did a good job at beating that out of me. Putting in my head that I'm worthless." I told him. I still have yet to look him in the eye. In fact I looked everywhere but at him. "Lucy your not cut out to be a cop. And I know I was wrong to set you up to get taken by a serial killer. And I can never explain how sorry I am. That's why I gave in and got myself in trouble and told them where to find you. Well what I knew anyway." I finally look at him. "Your sorry? Are you sorry I lost my unborn child? Are you sorry I didn't sleep or eat for almost 2 weeks. That I couldn't even shower because it reminds me of the barrel I was supposed to die in!!" I almost yell at him but I held the level down. "I'm here for closure Emmett. Not an apology. I'm here to tell you, you were wrong. I am brave, I am confident, and I will be the best cop in the whole damn road. I will take down every abuser, serial killer, and asshole that I come across." I look him dead in the eyes. "And I will picture you every time." I slam the phone down and walk out. Feeling a thousand pounds lighter. I get in my car and race to the psychologist. I run in tears pouring down my face. "I need to see Dr. Swan." "Let me call back and see if she's available." Her receptionist said. Thats when I heard, "come on in Officer Chen." She opened her door and I walked in. "I did it." She hands me a tissue, "thanks." "Did what?" She asks sitting down.   "I confronted Emmett. I told him he's wrong about me. That I am everything he said I'm not." I wipe my eyes. "Good. And what did he say?" "I walked away. I closed things on my own terms." I tell her. "I took charge of the situation. I stood up to him." I smile through my tears. "I feel so much better." I nod. "Well good. Now that you have made amends and came to terms with everything. I will clear you for active starting in 1 week. Then after 1 week I want you to report back to me and check in." I nod and get up, "and Officer Chen. I am so proud of you." She squeezed my hand.

Battle Wounds

1 week later   Tim's POV   I was in the kitchen at the station getting a cup of coffee. Today is the day Lucy comes back to work and insisted even though we live together we will drive to and from work alone until she graduates from being my rookie.

Nolan and West walk in the kitchen.   "So um- how is she? She's barely talked to us since the hospital." Nolan asked me. I take a drink of my coffee and look at them, "Well she made run out and buy her cover up at 4am. To cover the tattoo. She does that everyday. But she's doing better." I shudder at the memories of Lucy in her zombie phase.   "Well, wouldn't you? I mean, can you imagine walking around with a serial killer's brand on you? When can she have it removed?" West asked me.   That's when I saw Lucy walk in, she shot him a look, "4 weeks, 2 days and 9 hours." She then poured herself a cup of coffee.   "Hey for your first day back I figured you could use some sugar and carbs." We both looked at the plate full of donuts and scones Nolan was holding out. I took a bite and walked out of the room and to the bull pen.

I see Harper filling out some paper work and go beside her to grab a few things.   "So what's your plan?" She asks, I look at her confused.   "For what?"   "Officer Chen. I'm sure you've got some Alpha strategy, to get her "back on the horse." So, what is it?" She says with that Nyla Harper attitude.   "Your standard input overload. Force her to push through dynamic engagements. Hone in her fight-or-flight response." I tell her with confidence and skim through the papers I needed to sign off on before shift.   "So basically get her into as many fights as possible." She says.   "Well, I'm gonna remind her that she's a cop, the way she jumps at every sound and still has a hard time being a room alone. I need her to see she's not a victim. Because that's what she still thinks she is." "She knows she's not a victim. Look, Chen doesn't need to fight, she needs to make peace with the voice inside of her head telling her she's never gonna be safe again." I look at her with my are your serious face.   "Okay, I've been training rookies a lot longer than you. I know what she needs. You didn't see the way shes been the last 3 weeks." I tell her and close the paperwork and cross my arms. "That's ego talking. What happened to Chen is every woman's worst fear."   "Trust me, I'm aware of that. What happened to her is my worst fear for her." I say.   "But you have never lived that fear. It's clear that you have her best interests at heart. You may have been scared and looking for her. You may have held her hand through the mental recovery. But your weren't there, I'm just asking you to consider, whether she might be better served by someone who has been through what she has been through." Nyla tells me. She's not wrong... she really wasn't. I just wanted to be there for her today. But this is where I got to do what's best for Lucy and not me. "And that someone's you. Okay I'll talk to Grey and let me tell her, please. I don't want her getting the wrong idea." I walk to find those 2.

Lucy's POV Tim gave me a heads up that I'm riding with Harper today because she's been through something similar as me and that she could better help through my first day. He even admitted that he's probably not the best person to handle my first day back. I was disappointed but didn't let him see it. We are Rookie and TO not Tim and Lucy.

I get near the roll call room and pause. I asked Nolan to tell them not to clap me in. But I brace myself incase no one listens. I close my eyes and open the door. When I open them everyone is standing and clapping. I lock eyes with Tim who is smiling a little extra and he winks at me. I put my head down and rush to my seat. "Sorry I tried," Nolan says as I sit down. "Yeah, your dead to me." I tell him. "Welcome back, Officer Chen. How're you feeling?" Grey asks. "Can't wait to get on the streets, sir. Just get back to normal." I tell him, convincing myself as well as him. If I were tell someone I wasn't anxious for today I'd be lying. "So glad to hear that. We're gonna mix things up a bit. You're gonna be riding with Harper this week. Which means, Nolan, you and your ride-along are with Bradford."   After seeing a video of West on the red carpet we are dismissed.

I get the shop with Harper and we begin our patrol.   "You were right..." I look at her. "I was pregnant."   "I know, I was with Tim before he killed Caleb. And I'm so sorry for your loss." I sigh and nod.   "So whose idea was it to make the switch?" I ask looking around the area as we speak. "Mine but Tim agreed. You need someone whose been through what you have to help you get back into it."   I give her an unconvinced "Did you get set up to be taken by a serial killer by your ex and have your unborn child taken from you as well?" I asked her.   "Well, no." She had a flash of pity on her face.   "Well, then I'm not sure, how much help you'd be. But it's fine, 'cause I don't need any help. I've already worked through the trauma using both cognitive and exposure therapy, combined with mindful breathing, and Eye Movement Desensitization and Reprocessing, so it's it's fine." I snap at her. This exactly what I didn't want today, I didn't want to be treated different. I wanted to come to work with Tim and be treated the way I was before all of this.

That's I heard West radio in, "7-Adam-07, headed south on Hauser near 9th. Need backup for a felony car stop." I reached for the radio to respond and Harper stopped me, "You sure?" She asked "Hell yeah!" I said. "7-Adam-19, responding. We're approximately 30 seconds out, heading Northbound." I said.

Ready to dip my toes back in.   We arrive on scene and I see West surrounded by fan girls and his suspect running. I follow the suspect into a store. I wave all of the shoppers out, "get out of the store, get out of store," I yell loudly. The suspect fires of a few shots that I dodge. Seeing he is empty I make my move, "He's empty! Hey! Stop where you are! Police! Stop right there!" I get the suspect down, "Hands behind your head, fingers laced. Down on your knees. Control, show us one in custody. Code 4."

I arrive at the precinct and complete the booking process. Harper asks if I want her to do the paperwork, Tim would never ask me to do the paperwork. Today is just frustrating, knowing he wouldn't be going this easy on me.

"Abigail?" I see Nolan's future daughter in law and don't believe my eyes. We greet each other and I give her hug.   "I'm so glad your okay, did you get the flowers we sent?" She asked "And the basket. Thank you. So, you're Nolan's ride-along. How's it going?" I confirm with her and am quite shocked that she's doing a ride along.   "It's, uh, a lot." She says with a nod.   "Mmhmm." I say   "What the hell is this? I let you run around with Harper for half a day and you start hugging people on duty?" He looks serious. Hands on his side. I smiles, theres what I need.   "Don't listen to him he's all bark. I gotta pee." She skips off.   "All bark? She's not buying what your selling." I joke with him.   "That's because I don't hold her fate in my hands. Heard you dodged some bullets, are you doing okay?" "I just want to feel normal. She's going too easy. She offered to do my paperwork!" "Look, she's just being nice." He tells me. "Yeah, well I don't need nice, I need normal." I push past him. And I feel his eyes on me as I stalk away.

Later that day I am getting changed in the locker room. I look down and the tattoo is showing through. I hurry up and throw the shirt on before anyone sees. "Your not gonna shower?" Harper asks me. "Uh, no I'll do it at home." "We're not going home. Tim is going to get Lila for you and take her home with him, we are going to have some fun!" She points between her and Lopez and then to me. "Oh I get it, you've seen me on the job and your still not convinced." I say nodding my head and pursing my lips at her to show that I am not pleased. "No, that's not it. We just thought it would be fun." Harper holds her hands up in defense. "But if your not up for it-" Lopez turns to go. "Oh, wait, no, I am. It's - You guys have just never asked me out before without Tim being involved. But that's great. Uh, cool. So, where are we going?" I say.

We pull up to a bar and my heart stops. I'm not ready for this... "Guys, I-I'm not ready for this." I say turning around. "Oh no you don't, let's go. We got you." Angela stops me by my shoulders turns me around and gently pushes me towards the entrance. We get inside and get a table. Harper orders 6 shots of tequila and 3 beers. I look around and take in my surrounding. Mixed crowd, hip hop music on pretty loud.

There is 2 bathrooms, a bar taking up a whole wall. I next look for all the exits. Finding 3, the closest to me being 4 tables to my left.   I down both my shots and start sipping on my beer. "So, how was it to be back on the streets?" Lopez breaks the ice. "It felt good. I'm just ready to be back to normal." I say taking another mouthful of my drink and swallowing. "You know, I lost my TO on the job once and was off work for 2 weeks. I came back and I felt the same way. Ready for normalcy, then I realized it was never going to be the same again. Changed my whole way thinking." She downs her second shot. As the waitress brings us another round.   "Yeah, well my mission is to get every abusive asshole off the streets that I can." I down another shot.   "Harper?" She was looking around for a what I don't know. "What cha looking for?" I ask. "Nothing, let's go to the restroom. Buddy system." She nods and grabs my hand.   As we're walking someone touched my hips. I didn't think the next I knew I had him flipped over and pinned to the ground hand in the air. All eyes in the bar were suddenly on me. I let the guy go.   "Hey hey, it's okay." Harper puts her hand on my shoulder.   "You know, you really shouldn't touch a woman without asking, but, you know, we don't need to make a thing of it, right?" Lopez says to the guy.   "I was just trying to step around her without making her fall." He groaned.   "I-I'm so sorry." I ran to the bathroom and shut myself in. "Are you okay? What happened." Harper asked me. "I don't want to talk about." I grab my phone and call Tim to come get me. While I wait I go back to the table and take the round of shots sitting on table. Yep all 3 of them. I don't want to feel anymore. I chug my beer. "Woah, slow down Chen." Lopez grabs it from me. "Hey give that back. I need to not feel." I reach for the beer. "Not happening." She says. "Fine I'll go get another." I stumble to the bar. "Hey your kinda cute. Your the girl who flipped that guy earlier. Right?" A guy asks me. "Yeah, that was me." I ask the bartender for another beer. "It was kinda hot." He touches my shoulder. "Excuse me, but she's taken." Tim steps into view and grabs the mans hand a little too tight from the look on his face. "Scram or I'll have you arrested." He threatens. "Timmmm." I smile touching his hair. "What are you doing." He asks. I drink the beer that was sat in front of me. "Oooo Harper and Lopez brought me to bar and I embarrassed myself and now I'm drunk." I say like it's nothing. "Let's go. We're going home." "Don't be a party pooper." I boop his nose with my pointer finger twice on the last two words. "Bartender get this hunk a shot and a beer." "That won't be necessary." He says loudly and the next thing I know I'm over his shoulder and in the car. I fall asleep sometime on the ride home.

BEEP BEEP BEEP. "Make it stop." I moan from my sleep. "Time for work boot." Tim throws the covers of me. Wait covers? Suddenly I remember everything from last night. "Oh god..." I hold my head. "Remind me next time Lopez and Harper tell me they are taking you out, to tell them no." Tim says. "Remind me not to go. I'm so sorry." I tell him.   "It's fine. You needed to go in a crowd like that." He said.   "Yeah as embarrassed as I am, I feel like I won't be as nervous in a crowded bar again." I nod. He hands me a bottle of water and 2 Advil. I graciously take them. "Hey, I wanted to take you and Lila somewhere on our next day off... so don't make any plans." "Sure, what did you have in mind?" "Not sure yet. But we deserve a little family fun." He kisses me on the cheek. "I'll see you at roll call boot." And he heads out. "Come on Lila, time to go!" She runs down the stairs. After an uneventful morning Harper and I stopped at a store to get some coffee. Headed back to the car I see her staring at me, "I know what your thinking but I'm fine."   "You nearly broke that guys arm." We banter back and forth as we drive down the street when she finally tells me her story, "When you're undercover, you can't let go for even a second. You have to maintain complete control over your responses, read between every glance. It is physically, mentally, and emotionally exhausting."   "So what, you slipped and they figured out you were a cop? Or what?" Since she pulled over I looked her in the eyes. But see in her eyes what I see in mine anytime I think about Rose or what happened to me.   "I always met my case officer at a bar. It was the one place, that I could go where I could drop the character, and I could stop strategizing and just have a beer, and be myself. So, one night, one beer turned into two, which turned into – Well, I lost count. And if it were any other scenario, I would have sobered up, I would've cut myself off, but I wasn't with the crooks. I was with another cop. And I trusted him."   To say I felt like an ass was an understatement ... "I am so sorry." "Yeah, it was a long time ago, but my point is, I shut down. I didn't even tell my husband. I just, I kept telling myself that I would deal with it when I was ready." She told me... "But with every passing week it just got worse..." I finish for her.. knowing that feeling all too well.   "Maybe I pushed you too hard, last night. But I know what it is like when you do not face things head-on," I felt myself going back to the dark place I was in not just a week ago... my thoughts going to back to what I lost. What I went through... knowing I will never get justice for Caleb... I am glad Tim got to be the one to take him out. But the thought of him rotting in person does sound appealing. "Hey." She says snapping me out of it.   "Yeah?" I ask her...   "You will get through this." She grabs my hand squeezes it giving me a sad smile.   "What - What happened to him? Your case officer."   "He fell down a few flights of stairs and had to take a disability pension." I smile knowing how that happened but not saying it out loud.

We headed for a back up call in a trailer park. We arrived on scene to bullets flying, but they quickly stopped. We arrived late to the party   I saw 2 straggler/ trying to escape and immediately took action, "Stop where you are! - Down on your knees. Hands behind your head, fingers laced. Don't move. 7-Adam-19, two suspects in custody. Code 4."

At the precinct after booking my 2 arrests and mounds of paperwork I run into Tim in the hallway.   "You got no quit in you, do you, Boot?" He asks. "No sir, I get that from you." "I don't think so. You walked in the door this way. It's what makes you so aggravating to train and so easy for me to love." He says and I laugh a little. "You on the streets is so different from off duty Lucy and I still love you all the same."   "Well, I guess you get the best of both worlds." I smile and and start to walk away when I hear Tim start to talk again so I stop. "Hey, I was thinking today and I got half a dozen scars. Bullet wounds, knife wounds, broken bottle. Then there's the ones you can't see Isabel's addiction, a dad, who would tune me up on the regular, losing the baby, almost losing you. And whether I like it or not, they're a part of me. I know that's the last part you need to get over.. I see you, you know? Still trying to cover it. Scrubbing at it til it's raw..."   I cut him off, "I-I know what you're trying to do, and I appreciate it, but this is different. I was tattooed by a sadist who etched my day of death into my skin. The day we lost Rose, and that's what I'll think of every time I look at it. " I tell him.   "But you didn't die. Okay? You lived. And now he's the one in the ground. But I'm not trying to tell you what to do with it. Okay, I promise. Burn it off, keep it, whatever gives you peace and I will love you either way. All I'm trying to do, is give you some perspective. You can choose to see that tattoo as your greatest failure. But I see it as proof that you're a survivor. It wasn't your day of death, Luce. It was the first day, of the rest of your life. And no one can take that away from you." I smile at him with tears in my eyes. God if I wasn't in uniform I'd kiss him.   "Thank you." I tell him. "I will, um, see you at home." He nods and heads to the men's changing room.

Sergant Bradford?

Today is the day Tim finds out where he ranks on the sergeants exam.... Lucy is happy for him. Boot not so much. He's the best TO a rookie could ask for, the thought of someone else finishing my training makes me nauseous. I would never tell Tim this. Today we are also following up on a 3 day old gang invasion case that is about to be out in the back burner. We are looking for leads to be able to continue looking for the answer. We went and talked to Nevin but he insisted that he didn't need help. So we went about our day told him where to find us if he needed help. Now we are going back to the station to see if there's any other cases fo follow up on. I keep dreading the results of the score... I really don't want to be trained by anyone else, I have the best and who knows who I'll get stuck with if he promotes before I'm done training. I shuddered at the thought of Smitty finishing my training, "so how does it work?" I ask Tim. "The sergeants exam?" He asks. "Do you get the stripe right away?" With all thats happened the last few months we never really discussed what this would mean... or how it works. "No. Passing the test is the first step. You only get promoted when a spot opens up. You're at the top of the list, might take a month or two. The lower you are, the longer it's gonna take. And for some, they'll never get a shot. Be taking the test again in two years." Sergeant Grey came up to us, "your home invasion victim was just assaulted. He's on his way to the ER right now." "Nevin? We just saw him." I shuddered at the thought of what might have happened. From what I've seen and learned Gangs are not very taken to the thought of people going to the straight and narrow. We took off to the hospital. "So, how do you think you did?" I ask getting in the shop. "I'm not sure. With.. um.. everything I kind of slacked on studying." "Hey I'm sure you did great. Your the best out there." I smile and we arrive to the hospital. Nevin was pretty roughed up but not willing to talk. But we got information out of Sasha his girlfriend. The gang wants him to launder money through the bakery and gave him 24 hours to decide. Tim wanted Sergeant Grey's input on what to do so we headed back to the station and to meet with Grey. After filling him in Grey gave us some advice. "The smart thing would be to get Nevin to launder the money. Use him as a CI to roll up Marquel and his whole crew." "Um, Nevin's trying to go straight. We'd be destroying that." I tell them. I don't like this, if he wants to go to the straight and narrow this could destroy that. "Yes, in order to put some pretty bad people behind bars. Look, it's a tough call, but... you're gonna have to get used to making those as a sergeant." Tims eyes kind of perked up and he looked at Grey, "the scores are in?" "The list just arrived. You're number 8 out of 140." "Yes! I knew it. Congratulations... Sergeant Bradford." I gave him the best Lucy happy I could. But the look on Tim's face meant he didn't fall for the fake enthusiasm. Dammit. "Not a sergeant yet. At eight on the list, it'll probably take six months or so." He said. "Actually, there's a position opening in North Hollywood. The captain there owes me a big favor. If you want, I can make it happen. You'd start in two weeks." I give him a shocked look, "T-Two weeks?" I still have over a quarter of training to go. No no no no, not Schmitty! "Uh -- Uh, can I think about this overnight? We need to talk about this." He looks at me and I smile because he wants to make sure we talk about it. "Yeah, of course. But there's no guarantee you'll get a better opportunity, if you pass this up" Grey says looking a little concerned but I ignore it. Once we get back in the shop Tim looks at me, "we're going to find Marquel, have a little chat." "Okay, hey look I know you caught that look, let me explain." "Not right now Boot." He says stern leaving no room for question. If we were Tim and Lucy I would not have stand down but right now I'm Boot he made that very clear. After we confronted Marques he made it very clear he was not okay with hurting his rep by letting Nevin slide. "What do we do now?" I ask sliding in my seat in the shop. "I don't know. We made our play, and we failed." He says looking defeated. "Wow. I never thought I'd see you give up that easily." "You got a path to victory, Boot, I'm all ears." He says with a little bit of anger in his voice that I've never heard before with me at least. "No, I don't, but you're the king of subversive tests and tricks. There's got to be some way to win by coming at this sideways." I tell him. "I got a plan." Tim says and heads in the direction of the station we get inside to everyone at there desks. "Listen up everyone!" Tim yells and everyone looks at him. "Ex-gang member Nevin Cooper who is trying to leave a gang, is being threatened into laundering money through a bakery he works for, Donuts and more. All I need from you guys is to make that place your go to donut shop. The gang would never want to launder money through a place with that much police traffic." Everyone said some kind of okay sounds good. "Wow... that was genius Tim." I say. "Thanks." He walks away from me.

Later that night I lay on the couch with Lila playing with her hair and Tim comes home. "Hey, brought dinner." He tosses a bag down on the coffee table. "There's a game on I'll be in the basement." "Tim we need to talk." "What Lucy." "I know you saw my look about you getting promoted. Let me atleast explain myself.." "Lucy is over the moon excited for you." I tell him. "Well you didn't look it." He snaps back. "Boot isn't, and not for the reasons you think... I want you to move up and do great things like you did today. But I still have training left to do and you are the best trainer there is.

Could you imagine if I got stuck with Smitty for these last few months?" I ask and he laughs a little. "No I couldn't... that sounds awful." "I'm sorry I got mad... I've been thinking about it all day anyway... Tim Bradford finishes what he starts and I'm not done training you." He pulls me in for a hug and kisses my forehead. "Gwoup hug!!" Lila comes in and latches on to our legs. "Get up here." Tim reaches down and picks Lila up and I wrap my around her as well. "I love you guys." I say. 3 days later "Ugh, I am so glad to finally be off." I roll over and face Tim in bed. "Oh yeah?" He starts to nibble on my jaw and place soft kisses. "Yeah." I raise my eyebrows at him and lean in to kiss him. The kiss deepens and Tim starts to run his hands up and down my body. A half hour later "Now that is a way too start off a day off." I say climbing out of bed. "Maybe instead of my morning gym work out you can work me out." He winks and we both laugh. I get in the shower and stare at my ribs. That's it. "Tim!" I yell. He's in the bathroom in seconds. "What's wrong?" "I decided... your right. This tattoo isn't a reminder that I failed. It's a reminder that I survived... it's a start of a new Lucy Chen." I say. "Im going to keep it... for now anyway." I say smiling and nod a little. "That's good babe. Im glad your seeing it my way." He smiles at me. "Now hurry up we got plans today." He kisses my wet forehead. A few hours later we are in Tim's truck Lila buckled in the back. "So what's this surprise?" I ask him. "What's the definition of a surprise?" He asks. "Stop Tim testing me." I laugh. We pull up to the Santa Monica pier.   "The pier?" I raise an eyebrow. "Mommy!! Look cotton candy!" She pulls both our hands and Tim laughs a little.   "1 please." I say and Tim pays the man and he hands it to Lila.   "Mmmmm sooo good." She smiles. We walk down and play various games on the pier. I beat Tim in basketball shots. He was not very happy about that. Lila and I fed the pigeons on the pier. We ate lunch and listened to the band. We spent our whole day here. It was the best day of my life. Rode the Ferris wheel. Lila hasn't looked so happy in a long time. It felt so good to see the smile on her face. And Tim oh god ... watching him help her squirt a clowns mouth with water was the cutest thing I have ever seen.   At the end of day we walked down to the end of the pier to watch the sunset over the water.   Tim dropped to one knee. Oh my god! "Lila, sweetie, can I ask you something." "Mmmm yes." She nods and smiles. "I love your mommy very much and it would make me very happy if I could marry your mommy. Can I ask her?" He's holding her hands.   "Yes you can." She hugs him with her little arms. God she's growing up too fast.   "Lucy, I went almost 24 hours thinking you were going to be taken from me forever. That day is the day I realized I didn't want to live my without you ever again... our relationship is something special you came in and you softened my rough edges, made me a better man. You and your daughter have relit a spark inside of me I thought was gone forever. And I want to have that for the rest of my life. Lucy Chen will you marry me?" He asks opening a little box . "Yes! Yes." He takes the ring out and puts it on my finger when he stands back up I fling myself into his arms and hug him like I'll never hug him again. Then I pick Lila up and have her join in on the love. "I love you guys so much." He says. I giggle and we turn to face out over the ocean and watch the sun set. We stood there wrapped up in each other till there was no sunlight left. Making small talk with Lila, laughing and just enjoying each other.

Dammit Lucy!

"Come on Kojo, come one." I whisper to my new furry friend as I walk in the door of mine and Tim's house. Lila is giggling as she follows up behind us. I let the dog of his leash once the doors closed and immediately darts toward mine and Tim's bedroom. "Hey! Stay, stay." Tim's is pleading with the furry thing as I follow him. By the time I'm to the room Tim is sitting up and looks deeply confused. I go over sit on the bed and hug Kojo ruffling behind his ears as I do so. "Kojo! Oh, Kojo, Kojo! Come here. Check this out. What's this? Ohh, what a good boy! Are you so excited to meet daddy? Aah! You're such --" "What is going on?" Tim asks me. "Okay so remember how I was looking into getting a dog?" I asked "No." Huh weird I could have sworn I told him. "Yeah, dogs are super helpful for trauma recovery. I filled out the applications to foster Kojo, and they just dropped him off." I tell him and Kojo starts to whimper. "Oh it's okay, your a good doggy." I say rubbing his ears again. "No way. Nope.

Tim Bradford doesn't do dogs." He says. "Please." I say giving him a pouting face. "Pweaseeee Tim." Lila copied me. Good girl I raised you right. "Fine. But off of my bed." He shoos the dog away. "Yayy!" Lila dives into Tim's arms and hugs him. "Thank you. Thank you. Thank you!" I smile at them petting Mr. Kojo.

We are walking around courtyard in uniform and Tim looks distracted. "Are you mad about the dog?" I ask him. "No." He huffs. "Then what's wrong." I put my hand on his shoulder. "Nothing." He nods at the door we need to knock on. I knock on the door, "police." A nice dressed man opens the door looking quite annoyed. "You're too late. It's gone." I ask. I assumed there was a person spying. "It's?" I look around for some kind of clue. "We got a call about a Peeping Tom?" Tim is confused as well. "Wendy loves to tan in the morning. Last few days, this drone has shown up hovering overhead, spying on her." The guys seems really angry. "Well, we can put out an alert, but drones can be tricky to track down." He says and he's not wrong. "It's bad enough guys are constantly hitting on her whenever we go out. Now she's not even safe in her own home? You guys don't believe me? There's like a gravitational pull Wendy has no control over." I hold in laughter. I'm assuming Wendy, who is dressed in bathing come walking over swaying her hips. Looking up and down Tim. I again contain a giggle by swallowing. "Honey?" She drapes a hand on her husbands shoulder. "They say they can't do anything about the drone." She smiles wider and stares at Tim and give her what one could call a seductive smile. "I'm sure that's not true. The next time I tan... you can come watch." She gives a very subtle wink. "Ma'am --" Tim has a shocked lock on his face and I just turn and his my smile. "Are you hitting on my wife?" Barry starts to accuse Tim. "What? No!" He says quickly. "Get the hell out of my house!" Barry roars and points out the door. "Sir --" Tim holds his hands out to show he means no harm. But Barry isn't having it and I'm out the door behind Tim laughing once Barry slams the door. "Stop." He holds his hand up and I stop laughing quickly. "Are you hitting on my wife?" I joke. And once were in the car Tim cracks up laughing with me causing me to laugh harder. I look at my phone and check the cam I put up to keep an eye on Kojo. "Tim we got to go to the house." I say. He raises an eyebrow at me. "Not unless there's a crime boot." "No im serious look!" I show him the video and he flips on the lights and sirens and peels out to the house.

We get there and I race to the house Tim on my heels and the perpetrator jumps on my shoulder and licks my face. "Oh, no. Oh, my God. Kojo, what did you do?! Get -- Get down. Just..." I try pushing him down. "Sit." Tim demands and Kojo sits. "My favorite sneakers." Tim holds them up. "Ummm what do we do?" I ask. "I have a cage from my old dog in the basement I'll get it. I knew I should have said no." He rubs his head and walks away.

We got Kojo situated and head back on patrol.   "Tim I'm so sorry. He destroyed your house. I will call the company to come get him. I should have asked." I look at him and his hard face softens.   "I... I'm sorry." "Stop." He says sternly. I stop talking. What comes out of his mouth next almost floors me. "1. It's our house. 2. There's no reason to do that, you think he'll help you and make you feel safe. Fine. He stays. Stuffs replaceable your happiness is not." "7–Adam–15 in foot pursuit of suspect. 29100 Spring. White male. 160 pounds. 5'8". Green jacket. Send backup." Nolan calls in.

That Call lead Tim to reuniting with someone who used to serve Wes. He had somehow managed to get himself wrapped up with The DIA who were making counterfeit money. Against Sergeant Gray and the higher ups wishes Harper, Nolan, Lopez and I called LA CLEAR to get more information on the case to find that out. One of the workers confronted Nolan at his house allowing Tim to get a tracker on his car and led us right to the money. We did the take down successfully. But Tim and Harper had tons of paper work to do.

That night I have my head on Tim's chest. "Can we talk now?" I ask drawing small circles on his chest.   "Lucy, can we not... it's been a long ass 2 days." He twirls a piece of my hair around his finger. "No your willing to put your career on the line for this person and if I'm going to help. I should know to." I really will help him do anything but I need to know why. I hear Lila cry from her bed.   "I got her." He says and gets up taking the escape. I sit up and fall back on my side of the bed and let out a deep breath.   "Someone wants to join us." He comes in.   "Kojo?" I ask.   "Uh no dogs in the bed. But Little Boots are allowed and he playfully flies her to the bed and tickles her belly.   "Hi mommy I missed you guys." She kisses my face and settles between us. "I missed you too baby." I smile at her but give Tim a this isn't over look. "Night my favorite ladies." He turns the lights off and is soon snoring.

Hi. I'm Valerie Castillo. I work for the Los Angeles Herald. I'm here to see yesterday's case reports. CHEN Okay. You a crime reporter? CASTILLO Um, not yet. I write for the Style Section, going on 15 years. Oh. But I'm over it. It's all been reduced to sex tips and celebrity gossip. You know, the clickbait. CHEN Mm, so you're fishing for a real story? CASTILLO Actually, I've already got one. Do you know anything about a bunch of robberies at five-star hotels? CHEN Mm, first I've heard of it. CASTILLO "Well, a concierge at the Borden told me that two guests were beaten and robbed there in the last few weeks. Now, neither victim want her to contact the police. When I went to other stations to look through the crime reports, I found three similar incidents in hotels around town." Oh my gosh this terrible. Poor victims, this is exactly the type of case I want to help her solve. Or solve for myself. Woman should never be beat, sex worker or not. There still human. "Is there a description of the attacker?" "No, because none of the men gave one. But the cases have to be connected."

This is very interesting. Now I want to look into it. "Yeah, I mean, it sure seems like it." "You know, you don't want the case reports." She definitely will get more information from the CAD reports, "There's actually a lot more information in the CAD printouts." I tell her "What are those?" Valerie raises an eyebrow at me and leans in. "Computer Aided Dispatch reports." I tell her. "Why are you volunteering to show her those?" Tim comes rushing up. "This is a reporter from the Herald, and these are public-facing documents." I tell him as I check him out in his suit. "Valerie Castillo." She introduces her self and sticks her hand out to shake his but he declines it. Well flat out ignores it. "They're only public-facing when asked for." He has his hand on the binder She smiles at me and says, "Can I see the CAD reports, please?" "Fine. Give 'em to her." He lets out a sigh and hold the bridge of his nose showing his annoyance. "Thank you. Not a fan of the press?" She asks leaning in to him a little. "Eh, Herald's got a bias against the police." He looks at the lady with his cop eyes. "No, we don't." She defends "It's implicit." "Unlike your bias against me." She shoots back. "Cute. You know, the media will say or do anything to get you to back up their headline. And make sure she gives you those printouts back." He says sternly but his tone softens as he walks away. "And get ready to roll. We're gonna hit the streets as soon as I change." "Yes, sir." I say. "You shouldn't let him talk to you like that." Valerie tells me "He's my training officer. That's just kind of his style." I defend him because I know he's just doing his job. Outside of work he'd never talk to me that way.   "Well, being an ass isn't style. But he sure can wear a suit." I felt a panic of jealousy but ignore it and to meet Tim.

I'm telling you. Reporters always have an agenda."1

"7-Adam-19, 415-fight. Manager versus customer in a physical. Multiple RPs. E&L Auto Body. 3905.1" dispatch radioed in   "Copy that. En route, Code 3." I radio back to them and Tim flips on the lights and sirens. I get out of the car with enough time to see the customer pull a bright red snake out of its bag. My heart stops a little. "Like hell you will. Say hello to William Snakespeare, bitch!" "Hey drop the snake! Drop it." Tim orders but the guy doesn't listen and keeps taunting the shop owner. "Drop it!" Just then the snake does an in the air maneuver and bites the shop keeper. "Get that away from me!" The shop owner yells as we all get up off the ground. As the customer writhes in pain. "Oh no! Where the hell did it go." Tim and I both scan the garage.   "I don't know." He sighs. The guy on the floor still is screaming in pain doesn't look good, "Sir, just stay where you are. The ambulance is on its way." I assure him. "He's not gonna make it. Animal control's 10 minutes out. EMTs won't step foot in here until that snake's been neutralized." Tim tells me. That's just not right... "Damn it, well, we can't stay up here while he's dying." I look around for the snake again. "Alright, we'll just flush it out in the open. I'll end it." He reaches for his gun. HE WILL NOT!   "You can't kill it." I snap. "What the hell are we supposed to do with it? Snuggle?" He asks. Cute. I jump down off the car. "Boot, don't be a hero. It's venomous. Lucy, stop please." I work my way around the shop looking under things when I see the snake hiding under a car and it hisses at me. Shit. What did I get into? I look around for something to grab it with. And I see a long looking hook. "Hey, there, Snakespeare. It's okay. I'm not gonna hurt you. I just..." I slide the metal piece under the car, please don't bite please don't bite me, I inwardly beg as I hook it successfully depositing it into a stack of tires and putting a sheet of metal on top of it for good measure. "Hoo! It's not his fault his owner's an idiot." I look at Tim and relief floods his face. "Control, advise fire and ambulance our scene is Code 4 — clear to enter." Tim radios in. Once the owner is situated with the EMTs we get back in the shop. "You know that was reckless." He says. "Tim, don't. Please. You couldn't kill that snake." "Okay then you didn't listen to me." He says. "You were wrong. That man could have died..." I would never forgive myself I didn't try to make the scene safe so he could get the help he needed. "You could have died." He says softly. "And that's what I signed up for to put my life on the line for other." I turn and look out the window to show him I'm done with this conversation.

Later on when I'm about to off shift, I bump into Valerie the reporter again. "Mm-hmm. Valerie. Hey, you're back." "Hey. Yes. To thank you for getting me those CAD reports." Time to dig for some info, if I have enough of a lead or information Tim might just let us look into the case.   "Yeah. Well, did they help with your story?" I stared at her with my doe eyes wanting to know.   "You're kidding me. It's even bigger than I thought. You know, every one of those assault victims lives in town. Who gets a hotel room in the same city that you live in?" People who sleep with prostitutes, DUH! "Uh, well, men who are hooking up with sex workers." I say as if it's obvious... "Exactly. I'm convinced it's a Murphy scam. You know, the rich guy meets an escort at the hotel —" I know this!!   "Yeah, and gets beaten up and robbed by her accomplice but can't report it because then he'd be copping to his own crime." It's terrible.. "This was the story that I was looking for and my editor said to run with it and I couldn't have cracked it without you. So I want to buy you a drink to say, you know, thank you." Ehh— should I really trust her?   "Oh, uh, I shouldn't." No because I want to go home to my daughter and said TO but, I can't tell her that. And I could get more   "Why? Because your training officer would disapprove?" She looks around probably looking for Tim...   "Uh, no, no." Yes yes.   "Okay, listen, listen. You helped me, and I want to return the favor. So any time I get any information on crimes, I can feed it to you, and you can make the arrests." That's a hell of a deal.

At a hotel later we were discussing what information she got...   "It's exactly what I thought. He hooked up with a woman online. They went to a hotel, they go upstairs, they get naked, then a guy walks in with a gun. He steals the guy's watch, money, phone, and then tells him, "If you talk, your family's gonna get hurt."" "Did you get a description?" "Better. He gave me the woman. Now we're gonna catch her in the act." Um WHAT!! "Um.. we— um... Y-You lied to me." I told her... Tim was right! "No. No, I-I didn't. I told you I was gonna help you, and this way I was gonna get a killer story and you were gonna get a high-profile arrest." That does sound nice. "I'm a rookie. I can't just run around arresting people by myself." I explain to her. "Come on. Why not?" Her eyes snap to somewhere behind me, "Holy crap. That's Alex Shaw." She gasps and grabs my arm. "Who?" I'm so lost... "The huge movie producer. And his wife is super pregnant. This is suddenly a front-page story.This is amazing! Oh, no, no, no, no. They're gonna leave. Let's go." She is looking at a nice dressed man and woman who are walking towards the lobby. "What?" I ask... "I booked the room right next to hers. Come on! Let's go, Lucy." Valerie was pulling at my arm. "Lucy." I heard Tim's voice and snapped my neck in the direction it came from. Oh shit. "Tim I can explain. We were just having a drink when this happened!" I gave him the run down of what we found. "I'm in trouble aren't I." "Of course not. Boot is in trouble. Not Lucy." He softened his voice. "Huh?" "We.." and Tim cut me off. "Don't you dare tell her. It'll be front news." I pretended to zip my lips shut. I mouthed Lila? And he mouthed back, Wesley. I nodded.

We walk to the room and Castillo was spying with her phone.   "So is Shaw really in there with an escort?" He asks. "Yeah but there's no sign of her accomplice." I tell him. "Maybe he's not coming. Maybe he doesn't exist." Tim shoots Valerie a dirty look.   "He exists, okay? And when he comes, he's gonna be armed and dangerous." She smiles at him.   "If so, you'll be nowhere near the action." He tells her crossing his arms in true Tim fashion. "7-Adam-19, requesting another unit to the Coldwater Hotel for a 647-B event. Contact me in the lobby." He radios in.

"That's him. And he's armed. Dispatch, be advised, suspect at my location is armed with a handgun. White male, 6'2", black jacket, blue jeans. Here we go. Alright, stay... Where is she?" We both look around   "I don't know." I continue to look around when suddenly I hear a distress sound from the patio. "Ah! Aah!" We both run to the sound of her distress to see her dangling from the side of the building phone clutched to her chest holding on with hand for dear life.   "Hang on! He's running!" He looked through the window and I followed his gaze, the gay saw the commotion and was making a run for it. "Give me your hand! Let go of the phone!" "No, no, no, no! I have a photo of Shaw in — in bed." She's dangling and sounds scared. Is that picture really worth it?   "Valerie, drop the damn phone!" A picture isn't worth it !   "Give me your hand! Come on! Let go! Let it go." She drops her phone and he grabs her hand and pulls her up with ease. Pushing her towards me "Watch her. 7-Adam-19 in pursuit of the suspect, heading to the lobby."

Wow tonight was thrilling... not being known who I was. Taking down the bad guy in the end. Being used by a reporter not so fun.   "Lucy, what you did was stupid. You could have been fired, or killed!"   "I know." I say and look down. "I liked it though, being undercover.. no one knowing I was a cop." "No, don't even go down that road. No." I knew because of what happened with Isabel he was not a fan of undercover work.   We pull into the house and walk in.   "Well how'd it go?" Wesley asked.   "Ask Tim." I stomp off and close the bedroom door.

Tim's POV "Beer?" I ask Wesley reaching in the fridge for one. I see ponytails in his hair and laugh at him, "nice hair, dude."   "Dammit, Lila," he said as he reached up quickly and pulled them out.   "Sure." He said, "What's going on?"   All I can think about is watching Isabel fall down the rabbit hole, going in too far becoming addicted to drugs. It was hell... "Lucy expressed interest in becoming a UC." I chugged half my beer.   "Oh that's great." I shot him a dirty look, "or not." "No it's not, I can't go through that again. Not with Lucy." I shake my head to erase the images of all the pain she's already been through . "Lucy is not Isabel... I can't say she won't fall down that path, but I can tell you she's stronger than that." Wesley nodded at me.   "Tim? Where mommy?" Lila came padding out in her princess Pjs.   "Mommy's in our room sweetie. I'll take you to her." I pick her up, look at Wesley and tell him, "I'll be right back." "No it's fine, I should head home." He says pointing towards the door. "Goodnight." "Thanks again." I tell him. "Sure, she's great." He smiles. "Yes she is." I kiss her cheek and walk to the bedroom. "Mommy!" Lila dives from my arms to Lucy. "Hey sweetie, what are you doing up?" She tickles her little belly. "I wanted you to tuck me in." I smile at them because they really are my everything. "Sure thing, I'll be right back." Lucy kisses my cheek and I smile. Kojo follows them, "got you wrapped around there fingers too?" I say laughing. "Tim we need to talk," she walks back in, "I am not Isabel, I can do undercover work without falling down the rabbit hole." She looks at me hurt . "What about Lila? You saw what happened with Nyla and her daughter." I couldn't imagine what would happen to Lila if she lost both her parents. "Okay I only do short term UC ... small ones. I know I'm a mom. But if I can help out somewhere I want to be able to do it." "Lucy... you know how I feel about this." I tell her because I don't like this "And I know I feel about this. So I guess where at a disagreement." She huffs and pull the covers over me and turn away from me and it breaks my heart. "Seriously. That's how your going to end this?" I stare at her form "I guess so. Neither of us are going to win this argument. I still have a while before I can even think of going over cover alone. So no need to fight now. Goodnight." "Lucy, I love you, I'm sorry." I tell her not sure if she heard.

Lucy and her strays

"Okay, all done. Armstrong's energy is no longer welcome in this home. But if you feel it coming back, just call me. There's a more intensive treatment I can do." I was smoke treating Johns house to get out all the bad energy from everything that has happened to him. "Ah, that sounds awesome, but no, actually, this is -- this is good." He looks around and smiles. "You know what? We should really cleanse the station." I laugh I mean Armstrong was there a lot. "Oh, trust me, that process is already under way. They've reassigned about a third of our officers to other divisions, bringing in a bunch of new blood." What? How did Nolan know this and not me... "Word is, my new T.O. is from Valley Bureau." Lopez was recently promoted to detective so West has been bouncing round and round. Until now apparently. "Man, it sucks that Lopez couldn't finish your training." I liked her, she was good for Jackson. "Yeah, but I'm psyched for her. I mean, being a detective is all she ever wanted." If only Tim would be excited about what I wanted. "On the bright side -- even if your new T.O. is a nightmare, you've only got 25 days till you graduate." Don't remind me! I am going to miss being partners with Tim. "You should be moving up with us. It is not fair that Grey's holding you back. That letter of reprimand was severe enough." I tell John, after all the drama with Armstrong being dirty he got wrote up and can kiss his chances at ever being more than a patrol officer goodbye. "I screwed up. Actions have consequences. But when you graduate, you have to celebrate. No more Tim Tests? Come on." Yeah but I still have to deal with him at home.. don't get me wrong he's a great guy... but ever since I told him I want to go undercover he's been being different... great but different. "He's been quiet lately. Too quiet. He's planning something." I'm nervous... oh no! "Definitely. Where's the paint?" Jackson asks. "In the car." I point to outside. "Uh, your cars not out there..." Jackson says. We go outside and sure enough it's gone. "Did you lock it?" Nolan asked me. "Sure blame the victim." I can't believe him... "It doesn't technically lock okay!"

I call Tim, "I have an issue. Someone stole my car." "That hunk of junk? Cut your loss and we'll go get you another car when we're off next." "Tim." "Fine, when you get in for shift well fine a report. But I think someone did you a favor." "Did you get Lila dropped off okay?" I ask him. He let me come help Nolan and said he'd take care of Lila this morning and I was super grateful. "Yeah, see you at work." "Bye." I hang up and sigh. "Whose driving me?" I ask. John holds his keys of and nods his head towards his truck, "let's go." "Thanks."

We are on a call for a drunk guy who won't get out of his Uber. "Sir, get out of the car." "Can you please stand on the sidewalk?" Tim asks the woman who is standing over my shoulder. "Don't hurt the car. It's my only source of income." She pleaded with us. "What is the goal of this call, Officer Chen?" Tim asks me. "To get the Mountain's ugly cousin out of the car." I look at him as if it's obvious. "Wrong. It is to get him out of the car without making things worse. Now, do you think you can get him out without relying on your weapons?" He asks. I knew it! Tim test time. "Really? A Tim Test right now?" I ask... "Our goal as police officers should be to de-escalate whenever possible." He ignores my comment. "This from the guy who set me up to fight a suspect on day one?" I point out... and remember my take down that amazed Tim fondly. "Does this mean you're not up to the challenge?" He taunts me. "As a UC you'll have tons of challenges." "No, sir. I am game for whatever you want to throw at me." I raise an eyebrow at him. "Great. So, here's the deal. You start with 100 points. Reach for anything on your belt, and you lose points. Baton is 10. Taser equals 15. If you take out your gun, that's 50. Leave this call with 85 points or less, and you lose and I write up a blue page on you. Getting one of those at this stage of your training would be a real problem." Now where can I earn back points? "Can I earn points?" I raise an eyebrow at him and purse my lips.   "Absolutely. You get him calm, 5 points. He agrees to get out of the car, 10. You get him to apologize to the driver, 20 points. But if you use any of your weapons, game over -- you lose." "Back up. I got this. Excuse me. Hi. I'm Officer Chen. What's your name?" I push past Tim to the open window across from a very large drunk man .   "I want the pretty girl. Where'd the pretty girl go?" Uh rude.. I'm pretty just ask my partner back there.   "Well, she's right out here. Why don't you come out and see her?"   "You're trying to trick me. They told me all about that in the Marines." Okay this I can play on. Psych 101 find the weak point and play on it. "You're a Marine?" "Two tours in country. Oorah." He belches loudly and I grimace. "Thank you for your service. Why don't you get on out and let the pretty girl have her car back." I smile at him and point my head in her direction.   "Don't tell me what to do." He gets up quickly and moves me for me. I reach for my tazer in fear. Dammit! "Ooh! That's 15, Officer Chen. You're already in the loss column." He's enjoying this... "Let's go out." I help him move a little and close the door. "Eat a bag of d--" pretty lady says... and I cut her off.   "Not helping." I shake my head no at her.   "I'm not a bad guy." He starts to get emotional.   "Sir, look --" I go to comfort him and he flinched away.   "Back off!" He tells me.   "Okay. Okay. Look, I get it. It's been hard being home, back in your life, where nothing feels normal. But she's just trying to do her job. And I know your mother didn't teach you to disrespect women --" he cuts me off and gets angry.   "Don't talk about my mom. She died when I was over there." Grief is a bitch... "I'm so sorry. You know she would tell you that you're better than this. You fought for freedom, and that includes this girl's freedom from you harassing her 'cause... 'cause you got drunk and lonely." I play on what his mom would want.   "You're right. I'm sorry." He tells me... time to get 20 points.   "Don't apologize to me." I gesture to the driver with my head.   "I'm sorry." He turns to her.   "Bite me." I give her my best what the hell look. "Fine. Thanks." She looked so annoyed.   "Do you live here, sir?" He nods his head yes at me. "Alright. Head on up, straight to bed. And just take it easy next time you're at the bar." "Calm, plus leaving, plus an apology. I crushed this test." I do a little yeah! Move. And turn to the lady.   "Nice recovery." He smiles approvingly at me.   "Have a great day, ma'am." He goes to get in the shop.   "Oh! Uh, just wait one second." I pull out my missing car flier and show it to her, "Have you seen this car while you've been driving around?" I ask her hopeful. She does know where it was a little while ago and i take the directions and get Tim to head to the location.

We spot the car and someone in it. Tim flips the lights on and I jump out of the car.   "Stop right there! Put your hands on top of your head. Fingers interlaced." I say to the car jacker and handcuff her.   "You are under arrest for auto theft." I tell her.   "No. You don't understand. I didn't steal the car. The guy who owns it lent it to me, but he lost the keys." Ha! She's in for a surprise. "I'm the guy who owns the car." I tell her and she turns around to look at me she looks young. "You didn't even lock it. What did you expect?" She asked me... damn kid. "Yeah, well, it doesn't lock." I tell her as I set her down and Tim starts to bag her stuff up. "It does now." She tells me, what! Bad ass. We discover that she 17 years old, her parents passed away and she's living in my car. When Tim drops her stuffed animal she gets defensive about it and I set it beside her. She was just a kid looking for a safe place to say... I get that. "Uh...I-I'm not gonna press charges. Here, stand up." I uncuff her and tell her we will set her up at a children's shelter for now she said her stuff has been stolen too many times and it's too far away from school. "You still go to school?" Tim whips his head around to look at her and his eyes are the softest I've ever seen them on a call. And my heart aches for this girl. "Yeah. I do. And I get good grades. Any more dumb questions?" She is feisty though... Im not ready for this phase with Lila. "Look, I don't want to make getting to school hard for you, but I don't have a choice here, so it's either jail or the shelter. But I won't just dump you there, okay? I'll -- I'll help you find a permanent place." I will I mean it. I need to help this girl. "Is she for real?" She looks at Tim. "Officer Chen, a word. You, stand here, hands on the car." He has the girl stand by the car. "Congratulations." "On?" I look at him confused. "Your first puppy. Every rookie adopts a puppy at some point -- someone they think they can save. Honestly, I'm surprised it took you this long. She almost had me too. But the attitude." "Hey this could be Lila someday Tim." "See you need to stop. She stole your car Chen." "She is scared and alone... she still goes to school! Look I just want to find her somewhere safe to stay. And I'll leave it be." I explain to him. "Sure. And when your undercover and a teenager comes to buy drugs are you going to blow your cover to help them?" SERIOUSLY! He can't just let me be about my choice... "Tim leave it alone. We will talk about this when the time comes." "I'm just making a point boot." Now he's booting me... "Well for your information, I would never jeopardize my cover on purpose, no matter what. Now let's go." I jerk my head back to gesture towards Tamara.

That night I go home and Tim is going to do his nightly workout and meet me in a hour. I start preparing dinner and talk to Lila aimlessly about princesses and Harry Potter. She also asked me to take her to the beach. I never took her before because of Emmett and the bruises so I tell her I can make it happen and now she's talking about seeing mermaids and sharks... oh my baby is perfect. Kojo starts barking causing Lila to jump down and go to the door. "TIM!" She screams and jumps in his arms. "Hey my girl. How was your day?" He asks sitting her down. "Mommy said we can go to the beach and swim in the ocean! I think we're going to find a mermaid!" "That sounds perfect." He pats her head and makes his way to the fridge and pulls out a bottle of water and sits down. "Smells good. What's for dinner?" He asks. "Stuffing and chicken. I'm feeling carby." "Okay. I'll be in the living watching the game." He gets up and heads that way. "I watch?" Lila asks he nods and she squeals and follows. "We'll just you and me Kojo." I pat his head and turn my attention to one of my law books to study for my upcoming test. Tim and Lila watched the game and then I sent her to bed and I sat down beside Tim. "You know, I don't like how your being about me saying I want to go undercover. And to bring it up at work like that." I finally give in because I can't take the tension any longer. "Just tell me you'll decide to specialize somewhere else and I'll leave it be." He holds my hands in his and looks me in the eyes. "Tim it's what I want... and if you can't realize that I guess we aren't as meant to be as we thought. And I really don't want that to be the case. Can't we compromise when the time comes." "How so?" He sits back and folds his arms. "How about I run past you the case before I do it. And I promise I won't got on long term cases. I can't leave Lila that long." "Deal, kiss on it?" He raises an eyebrow at me and leans in. "Deal." And with that we kiss. It deepens quickly and he has me up with my legs wrapped around him in and is carrying us to our room.

The next morning I woke to a. All about Tamara informing me that she left the children's center in the middle of the night. "You got to be shitting me." I say loudly while I'm brushing my teeth and Tim's showering. "Tamara, left the children's center." "What did you expect babe, she's your puppy." He laughs at me "I just want her to be safe! She's not a puppy she's a teenager!" "She stole your car!" Quit reminding me! "Yeah yeah yeah. I'm going to get Lila ready." I say.

"We are not going to find her." I'm currently trying to talk Tim into going to the school for a welfare check. I looked her up at the station before roll call and found her school. "Please." I put on my puppy dog eyes. "Fine but if we get a call we are leaving." He says firmly. "Deal." We drive over to the school and I see her immediately. "You can take me back to the shelter, but we both know I won't stay." I know she won't... and it sucks. She deserves better than this. "I know, but living on the street isn't any better. You know, you deserve more." I tell her... ugh if she has my car she can stay at the shelter and get to school. "There isn't more. There's just this." Ouch my heart... stop it. But I know it isn't true. If she didn't have hope she wouldn't be trying to finish school and working so hard. "You don't believe that. Otherwise, you would have given up, dropped out. I think you believe that there's something better out there. You just need someone to help you find it. So, look, um... I'm gonna give you my car." "What?" Tamara and Tim say. "Boot." I look at Tim and hold my hand up. "You've been telling me to get a new car since I met you. So respectfully that's what I'll do and I'll someone else out with mine." I hold out my key. I told her that in order for me to do this she needs to check in with me so I know she's okay. And she stays at the shelter til I find her a safe home. She agreed to the terms and thanked me a bunch of times. "Well add car shopping to our list for our day off." I joke with Tim when I get the shop. "If I had know you would give that hunk of junk up for charity I would have found a homeless teen months ago."

Chenford Undercover

After getting sent to do some security at a undercover convention Tim lectured me about ease dropping on thing we were supposed to... apparently the seminars are strictly for UC only. If I had been caught by anyone but him I would be in big shit. I actually was listening to Nyla's lecture.

At end of shift I jump into no other than Harper herself. She saw me to, this is going to be fun. "Hey," she walks up to me with a knowing look on her face. "Hi." I wave a small little wave to her, feeling awkward." "So, you know we're gonna have to talk about it, right?" She says leaning against the wall. Look, it was a momentary lapse in judgement, and Tim has already scolded me for listening in, but I gotta say, um, what I heard at your seminar was amazing." I recalled the conversation and shuddered a little. "I was a little rusty, but thank you." "Listen, I've been thinking a lot about what I want to do once I'm eligible to test, and... I think I could be really good at undercover work. I would love to pick your brain sometime

-- not about tactics, just... what I should focus on to prepare for the job." I explain nervously. "I actually -- I...have time for drinks right now, if you want." She gestured to the door with her thumb. "But no tequila for you!" I laugh recalling how much I had last time she took me for drinks.   "Yeah. Great. All right. Uh...no. I have a homework thing with Tamara. She won't mind if we do it a little bit later. Let me just give her a call. Oh and Wesley, Tim won't be home for a few hours and Lilas babysitter will need relieved!"

Harper answers her phone as it's ringing and put her phone on speaker.   "I'm in a bind. Look, the real reason I couldn't make the convention today is because I spotted a tail on my way down from Sacramento." Harper volunteers to go help her out and tells us she's in a Mustang GT and goes by Coco. "Sorry. I'm gonna have to call Grey now, and we're gonna have to take a rain check on our drinks, but —"   "Totally." I'm bummed but I get it. She's gotta help a friend/colleague out. "Unless you wanna come." She shrugs and gestures to the door. "You go in, find June. Remember, her undercover name is Coco. She's a friend in town. Buy her a drink, chat her up. I will hang back and try and spot who her tails are. "Coco?" I ask the girl who resembles the picture harper sent me. "Hey." She says and gestures to the empty seat at the table. "Hey. Harper found a tracker outside. We think they're here." "Yeah, I know. One's at your 4:00. Haven't spotted his backup yet." The waitress approached and order us both another drink.

When a man Asian man sits down and says, "make it three. Hey what a coincidence seeing you all the way down here." He smirks.   "Like hell. You followed me" she got spunk, just like Harper. Mental UC training note: get spunky.   "We got a lot of money on the line with this deal, so we need to be very careful. A lot of people in this business, you know... they don't have integrity." He shoots her a dirty look.   "Yeah, 'cause you're just filled with integrity, aren't you, Sato?" She sips her drink.   "Oh, you say my name in front of someone that I don't know? What is wrong with you," he looks at her furious and then to me, if looks could kill we'd be dead.   Time to put my spunk to the test, "No, what's wrong with you? No one asked you to sit."   "Who is this bitch?" I throw my water in his face. " Oh, you just killed yourself. I'm looking at an empty chair right there." He threatens me.   "Then who's gonna conduct the hydrogenation process? Who's gonna perform the molecular synthesis to get the acid tables balanced? You get that wrong, you're gonna have buyers with brain bleed." I threaten him... and hope to god he buys it.   "You're the chemist." His eyes get huge and then he looks to "coco" and points at me with a smile, "She's the chemist."   "Yeah, she is. Now back off. And tell your boss price just went up 5% for the lack of trust." Coco tells him.   "Oh, I don't think so. Let's take a walk, talk about this somewhere a little more private. Hmm? We're gonna go for a little ride. Think about why, uh, I got such a bad feeling about you." He gets close to her and whispers in her ear.

"These guys are cops. They put a tracker on your car." Harper came in holding the tracker and slammed it down on the table. "Got a bad feeling about me, huh?" Coco leans into him and gives him a look that could kill. "Hey, we're not cops." He seems so insulted. "You want me to do 'em here or take 'em to the farm?" Dude, I need to be trained by her next. "Hey, you gotta believe me. Coco, you know me"

They negotiate on prices and the whose dick is bigger game. While I sat back. She talked him up 10% of there original price.

"I'll call you on this phone with the new location. And you better pick up on the first ring. Now piss off." She she holds the phone up and points at it then the door. I sing Harpers praises and she told me to study up on chemistry because I'm going to be helping them tomorrow. "What time is it?" 10:30! "Shit! I forgot about Tamara. And Lilas been with Wesley and Tim! Shit, Tim!" I hold my hand to my forehead. I call Tamara first cause she'll be the easiest. She reschedules for tomorrow with me. Wesley said he left Lila with Tim around 10. So I call Tim who called me 4 times." "Lucy, where are you? Are you okay?" He sounds worried. "Yeah I got caught up helping Nyla with something. I'll be home in a hour or so and I'll explain." "Okay, be safe. And hey, don't worry me like that. I thought..." I cut him off before he can say it. "I know. I'm sorry I love you." I tell him. "I love you too." We hang up and

I have Harper drive me home since I haven't had a chance to buy a new car yet.

When I arrive home Tim and Lila are both asleep on the couch. I move Lila and it instantly wakes Tim and I hold my finger to my lips to show him to be quiet. "Where have you been? I was worried sick. No one knew where you were. I... I... you can't do that to me Lucy." Tim is on a rant. "I know, I know, and I'm sorry. I told Wesley I was getting drinks with Harper to talk about UC work and I ended up helping her and another detective out on a case." I sit down beside him. "Lucy," "Before you go all off on me, you got to know. It was last minute. I had no time to react. And truthfully I could let Harper go with no other back up." "I know. I'm sorry, I just... I went through for a half hour..." he pulled me into a hug and put his hand in my hair to tighten the hold. "I'm sorry," I reach up on my tippy toes and kiss him. "I love you." He says and kisses my forehead. "I love you too." He moved his hand to cup my cheek and ran his thumb under my eyelid.

"This is Sergeant June Zhang of Fresno PD. We are gonna help out on her op today." Harper introduces Zhang, "Coco" to everyone. "Appreciate the assistance, guys. I'm June, the UC. My case officer, Lieutenant Balasco, who is not nearly as mean and awful as he looks. For the last eight months, I have been up on a crew out of San Jose who made bank selling precursors of liquid Fentanyl. But they got greedy, tried to go from selling the parts to making and selling the finished product. But their lab blew up, killing their chemist and destroying their entire supply, leaving them with no product and a lot of pissed-off buyers." Which is when I swooped in, promising enough product to satisfy all their customers and then some. But last night, all our hard work almost fell apart, until the quick thinking of Officer Chen saved my ass." I smiled at her praise. "Chen, stand up so they can see what you're wearing." I stand up and show them me in my black shirt and jeans jacket so I don't get confused and get hurt. "The op today is simple. Trade drugs for cash, then arrest everybody and try to get them to flip on Aldo Salonga, their boss." Sounds simple enough. "All right. You have your assignment. Everyone in position by 10:00 a.m." "You can't pit an untrained probationary officer against one of the most dangerous crime syndicates in California." I knew Tim would have something to say. "I don't want to hear it, Tim. She volunteered. Plus, Grey authorized it, and we have some of the best operational expertise she could ask for." Harper shoots him down. Ugh, I forgot to mention this part to him last night and he shot me hurt look. "They know the gladiator cage you're walking into. You don't. That's not volunteering. That's being used." Harper stares him down, "fine, but I want in. Make sure my boot can handle herself." Maybe I can take this to prove to him I can do UC work and not get too deep. "And this has nothing to do with yours and Lucy's agreement with IA?" Zhang stares him down. "No. Ask anyone here, it has never once comprised our work or swayed my decision or training for Officer Chen. If it were up to me as her fiancée and not her TO she would be a million miles away from UC work." He's not wrong. Zhang and Harper both stare at him to read his expression. Then look to me and I give them both a small nod to show them I am okay with it. "Okay then. Go get changed. You'll be product security . They think she's the cooker." "I'll have on a black T-shirt and jeans." He tells everyone and heads to change. Tim's POV How could Lucy get me agree to being okay with her going on UC if we BOTH agreed to the operation. Then, turn around and volunteer to go up against one of the most dangerous drug dealers out there! She's nuts... I punch the locker after getting changed. Reckless. Impulsive. But I love her... I get it, Officer me gets it! She couldn't let Harper go alone last night and like they said if she hadn't jumped in the whole operation blown. Grey explained to me in the office what happened as my friend. So I had to play it off as clueless in roll call. "All right, uh, let's go over this one more time. Salonga's crew arrives, you test the Fentanyl, give them a show, we get the money, they get this van, and then, boom, strike team takes them down." Harper goes over it with Lucy and I. "Walk in the park." June says looking over me and Lucy. Clearly not okay with our situation. "And if not..." she cocks her hun. "...we make some noise until the cavalry arrives. You want to go over the signals again?" She asks Lucy. It's hard being on the sidelines and not doing the coaching but I listen and take it all in for myself. This never was my area.... It was always Isabels. Isabel is also why I'm not a fan of this... at all. But here I am backing my Boot. "Yeah. "Workhorse" means we're in trouble. And "Beautiful day," we're all good." Good job. "Lucy." "Mm-hmm." "Are you all good?" "Yeah. Yes." She nods. I don't believe it. "You know, if you're not nervous, you're not human. Okay? So, use this to your advantage." I look her in the eyes and read them as I speak to her and she smiles a little and nods at me. "Be scared. Be wild. Be unpredictable. Be a cobra." Harper hisses like a cobra and her and Lucy laugh. Hmmm, they would have made good TO/Rookie... maybe I should have switched when we admitted our feelings.

"Let's do this!" An Asian man walks up. Empty handed. "Where's the money?" Harper asks. Looking around. "First things first. I wanna test the shipment." He looks at Lucy with hungry eyes. "Hard positives on every scale. When's the last time you saw that? Never. There's nothing available this pure." Damn, I never knew she could be this good at UC. Police work, she'll be one of the best but playing a cooker, I never knew it. I get distracted from my thoughts by another vehicle pulling in, shit shit shit. The man walks over and takes a sample from the small bag Lucy is holding and nods in approval, "Now let's see the cash." Zhang demand He speaks into the radio, "we're in business." As he says that another van pulls up. "If this is a set-up, you're the first to go." I train my gun on the man. And then Harper follows suit. "Relax. It's just my boss. And he wants to talk...to you." His hands are up to show surrender but gestures to Lucy. "Me?" No, not Lucy... The window on the SUV rolls down and a man looks at Lucy and speaks. "Good morning. My apologies for last night. Sato overstepped. It won't happen again. Come in and talk to me." 2 henchmen get out and one opens the door for Lucy to get in. "Why?" She looks scared. She either is scared or is playing the part. I'm going to go with both though. The man laughs and says, "A monkey can be taught to test for drugs... or a cop. I need to see that you really know the science." Lucy looks at me and nods very subtle to show me she'll be okay. Lucy slides in and one of the men get back in with her . I look at Harper to asks what's up and she subtly shrugs that she doesn't know. But we both keep our eyes on that van. One weird move and we plan to come to the rescue. I stand there holding my breath every minute she's gone. Once she steps out with the cash, our cops pull in and bullets start flying. I let a breath of air and join in. They get the crews down and arrested. No one was shot. No one suspected Lucy, Harper or Zhang. They blamed the man from the start I still don't know his name.

Missing

It's a sunny day in Los Angeles as usual, I have 2 days left of training and Tim and I are out on patrol. "So which car are you thinking of getting?" Hmmmm... "Idk, I still haven't found the one." I shrug. "Lucy we've been to 3 car lots." He groans and I laugh at him. "You know I'm going to miss this." I say. "Oh really?" "Mmhmm, you and your Tim tests. But I'm excited to advance my career. And maybe a Sergeant opening will come up soon." I wiggle my eyebrows at him causing him to laugh. My phone rings, "oh, it's Mrs. Lopez, I better answer this," I say answering it. "Hey how's Lila?" "Sh-she I-I" she's stuttering. "Are you okay? What's going on?" Tim stares at me. "She's gone. We went to the park and I can't find her." "What park?" "The one on 5th." "Go to the park on 5th she can't find Lila." We flip the lights and sirens on. "7-Adam-19, requesting back up at the Wisendale Park. Missing child. Age 2 female. Dark hair, dark skin, brown eyes, about 2 feet tall. Should be wearing a pink t-shirt and jean shorts. Missing child's name, Lila Lang."   "Hey, I'm sure she just wandered off to play somewhere and Mrs. Lopez can't find her. She'll be okay." He grabs my hand and squeezes it but I can see the worry in his eyes.   "7-Adam-15, put us em route ETA 5 minutes."   We pull up and Mrs. Lopez comes rushing over.   "I-Im so sorry guys." She looks devasted. "Did you look everywhere in the park?" Tim asks her. "Y-yes." "7-Adam-19 to 7-Adam-15 shut down all exits to the park. No one comes in or out." "Start a canvas. Where was she last seen?" Tim asks. "On the swirly slide. She asked me for a snack. So, I came back to get it and when I went to the slide she was gone." She grabs a tissue from her bag and wipes her eyes. "I'm so sorry." I feel tears prick me eyes.   "Sergeant Grey comes up to us."   "We got all exits closed and units on the look out canvassing out 10 miles. I got 3 units here collecting statements. We will find her. Okay guys?"   "What can we do now?" I ask. "Start taking statements."   "Here's a picture, I keep in my wallet. If you want to start showing it around." Tim pulled the picture of The 3 of us out of his wallet from her 2nd birthday.   "Lucy are you sure you can handle this?" Sergeant Grey asks me. I feel him and Tim look at me.   "Im sure." I nod. And I walk over to a lady standing by the bench that Mrs. Lopez was at. She said she saw Lila on the slide and run over to the swings.

   "Officer Chen come here!" Tim tells from across the playground.   "Thank you for your time." I shake the ladies hand and make my way quickly to Tim.   "Yeah?" "Show this lady a picture of Emmett." "Uh okay?" I grab my phone and show it to her. "That's him. That's the guy. I didn't think anything of it because the girl willingly ran over to him." My heart stopped. "He's supposed to be in prison." I look Tim. "I know. Come on." "Thank you for your time and information, ma'am." Tim shakes her hand and we walk away. "I told the jail to contact me if he got released." Tim then clicks on "Sergeant Grey we need you. Meet me by the fountain." "Yes?" He comes up to us. "A lady gave a positive ID on Emmett Lang as taking Lila. Said he walked away quickly across the park to the back entrance. "Isn't he supposed to be in prison still?" "Yes and no one contacted me of his release." "Let me make a call. Advise units of the new information for me and send a unit to see if there's any cameras that may have caught them leaving or the car he was in." Grey grabs out his phone and walks a few steps away. "All units be advised, Lila Lang was last seen being taken by Emmett Lang on foot and exited the park at the rear entrance. Stand by for my information." That's when Nolan and Harper make there way to Lucy and I. "Hey, we need a unit to go speak to the local shops see if anyone has any footage pointing towards the rear park entrance. Try and get plate or even a car make and model." He tells them. "Sure, anything. How you guys holding up?" "Trying to keep focus. It's hard... I'm scared for her. She hasn't seen him in months." Lucy shakes her head and I put a hand on her shoulder. "Lucy... she will be okay. We will find her. Come on. Let's go see what Grey says."   We walked up to Grey and his face is full of shock, "Emmett escaped during the prison riot a few weeks ago." "Why wasn't anyone here informed? The news! Someone." Tim is angry.   "Slipped through the cracks. Unfortunately it happens. Probably was chopped up as a casualty." Grey shakes his head.   I walk over and sit on a bench, I'm breathing heavy, borderline hyperventilating. Tears pull over and I put my hands on my face and just let them out.   Tim's POV Red I am seeing red... that little girl, is as much my daughter as she is Lucy's. I love her with all my heart and soul, if anything happens to her I will not hesitate to kill him.   I am enraged to say the least that no one informed, the station, me, or Lucy. He tried to have her killed for petesake! I look around for Lucy and see her crying with her head in hands.   "Grey?" He looks up at me, "can we have a few Tim and Lucy moments?" "Of course. Get her to pull it together. Then go and help on trying to ID a vehicle." "Thanks." I walk over to Lucy and pull her hands off her face and hold them in mine. "Come here," I pull her to her feet and pull her into the best hug we could with our belts on. "Tim... we can't." She goes to push me away but I tighten the hug.   "It's okay. Grey said to take a few moments". She rests her head on my chest. I feel a few tears slip down my face as well.   "Okay. I got that out. Now what's the plan?" She asks and stands up straight wiping a few stray tears from her face. "Harper and Nolan are questioning the shops across the street and looking for a camera that would have seen them." I nod.

"I need to do something. I feel helpless." "Let's go help them." I nod in the direction of the shops. "Hey we were just coming to see what shops you spoke to." "We got a partial plate and car make model and color." Nolan tells us: "I work with this." Harper takes the information and looks over it.   "Call it in. Meet us at the station." I tell them. We go and talk to Emmett's mother and let her know what's going on. She said she hasn't heard from him and then she cries over Lila being gone Lucy comforts her for a few seconds and tells her to call immediately if she hears anything.

We arrive to the station and I see Wesley answering phones. "Hey, how's Lucy?" He asks me.   "She's being strong... I'm sure her minds going back to you know... losing the baby. Fear of losing Lila. Hell I'd be lying if I said I wasn't scared." I was honest with him.   "Yeah I've been here since I found out helping where I can. Angela even came in. She should be with Harper running the plate or something." "Thanks." "Well what do we got?" "A black Ford Fusion registered to a Nathan Lang."   "Emmett's brother." Lucy walks in and says she pulls her phone out and calls someone, "Mrs. Lang, has Nathan been in contact with you?" She ask Mrs. Lang there is a pause, "Can I send a officer out to get your statement about your last interaction?" Lucy nods at me and I go in the hallway and I find 2 officers I trust and send them with instructions on what to ask.   "Okay. So we got that. She says she didn't seem to indicate that anything was going on. So no leads."

She comes out to me and runs her hands through her hair. "Let's prepare a team to go to Nathan's house. I got the search warrant approved. No knock." "That is why I love you." I tell her. Angela stands up and we nod and follow. Lucy is being extremely quiet and I can't take it. At Nathan's house we park down the street and get in formation. Angela, the other officers, and I are going to breach the front. Lucy, Nyla and John and 2 other officers are going to breach the back door. "There is possibly a child in that home. You don't shoot unless your sure you have to and she is nowhere in sight!" Angela announces. Thank you!

Lucy's POV   I keep thinking about Rose... I know that's selfish and stupid right now I should be thinking about Lila but in a way I am. I am thinking about the hole Rose left that Lila being gone is ripping open again. I need to find Lila. She's my baby girl, my everything, if I were to lose her I would not come back. She's my reason for breathing. She's the reason I snapped out of my zombie state... if I lose her . I'm going too. Right now we are going to break down Emmett's brother Nathan's door. I hope she is here. "All units be advised, making entry." Angela's voice   We go in through the fenced back door. Nyla let me lead the line. As soon as we entered the fence I felt 2 arms grab viciously and before I could react my weapon was thrown and something hard was pushed to my head. Hand wrapped around my neck. "Anyone moves and she's dead." "Let her go." I hear Tim's voice say. "Where's Lila?" I croak.

Tim shakes his head to tell me she's not in the house. "Safe. I just used her as bait to get to you. I would never hurt my daughter. I'm not a monster." I scoff at him and he tightens his grip. "Now all of you better scram and get out of here... or I blow her brains out right now." He pushed the gun harder. "I'm not leaving without her," Tim steps up and I shake my head as much as I can to tell him no. He steps closer and Emmett shoots Tim in the shoulder. "NO!" I scream. As the gun goes back to my head "I said LEAVE!" Emmett screams. "I will get them back. You stay strong Lucy." Tim and the rest of the crew fallback. Once there out of sight Emmett drops me. "What do you want?" "To finish the job I had started. Then Lila and I are going to flee to another country. I'm thinking Cuba.. Maybe, Jamaica." He taps his chin. "I almost believed your apology in prison. How did you get out?" I ask from my spot on the ground. As he ties my hands up. "Well, that prison riot... Nathan was visiting. Once the riot broke out I beat him to death and changed our clothes. No one cared about the body enough to notice the subtle differences." He yanks me up and drags me in the house. "See you in a few hours." He hits me with something hard and I succumb to unconsciousness. Tim's POV "I'm not going to the hospital." I argue with Angela "Yes you are. Why? Because I'm sidelining you. This case hit my desk so there for I'm in charge. Go get looked at, clear your head as much as possible and I'll think about letting you in the recovery mission. That's an order." I punch the wall on my way out. "Hey, let me drive you." Grey comes up to me. "She's right in there. And no ones doing anything!" I roar at him. "You know there was no way to take him down without risking hitting Lucy." He tells me and we get in his car. "Air support is not leaving the area and we will catch a trail at some point. Lila wasn't there. He will lead us to her."   "So in the mean time, Lucy gets to be his punching bag?" I feel sick. "Pull over." Grey pulls over and I open the door and throw up. "You good? You know I'm not going to let you in on this til you calm down."   "This is twice now Lucy got taken by him and I had my guard down..." I shake my head. "Call me when your fixed up. I'll keep you updated." Grey pulls in front of the hospital and I get out and walk in. The only thing on my mind, is Lucy... she's gone again. I could lose her again. And Lila little boot, she doesn't deserve to be roped into this . She's an innocent child. I will bring them home and never let them go again.

Payback

Lucy's POV I awake to the sound of Lila crying. I look around and the room we are in is dark...   "Hey, come here baby." I say softly.   "Mommy." She crawls on my lap and lays her head on my lap. My hands still tied together I manage to get my hands on her head to play with her hair. "I love you sweetie. We will be okay." I let the tears run down my face as I remembered being tied up in a barrel not too long ago. But this time, I'll be stronger. This time my daughter is alive and in my arms. "I wuv you mommy." "Oh goodie, your awake..." Emmett came in with a devious smile. "Don't. Not in front of her." I say looking down at Lila. "Okay. Then get up and let's go." Please be looking for me... please. "Mommy no go." Lila pulled on my hand. "Mommy and daddy just need to talk. I love you sweetie. Never forget that." I kiss her forehead and Emmett pulls me away. "Well well, now I get my revenge." He smiles sickly. "Look, you don't have to do this." I try to plead with him.   "Oh yes I do, I'm looking at 25 years in prison for confessing to setting your ass up to be murdered..." He steps in front of me, "If I had known that I would never have told them what I did." He smacks me across the face. "I'm going to make this as fun for me as possible." He gives me a devious smile and leans in. "Ready to take back what's mine." I cringe at the thought of what he means. He shoves me on the ground and I try to fight back. With my hands being tied I'm almost useless. I kick my feet at him. Aiming for any skin I can make contact with I lay one in the man area and he swears and punches me in the nose and I succumb to darkness.

Tim's POV Thankfully the bastard shot me through and through. I was stitched up, given some pain meds and discharged. I called Grey and he sent Lopez to get me. "Now, I would tell you to go home and wait. But I know that's pointless and you'll just get in my way. Did you cool down?" She asked me driving. "Yeah. As much as possible." I nod. "Good here's a clean shirt." She tosses me a clean uniform shirt. I change it and toss the dirty one in her back seat. "So what's the deal? Did you find her?" "Yes, we'll sort of." She pauses and takes a deep breath, "air ship followed them to a wooded area. Where they left on foot. We have teams there canvassing the area looking for them. "Well let's go join in." "I thought you'd say that." Angela smirked, "Detective Lopez to Air Control badge number 29842 we are ready for pick up. Officer Tim Bradford badge number 34831 accompanying me." We board the helicopter and it takes off. "Stay low to the trees and drive slow." She tells the pilot. "Copy that." "Here put this on. For when it's time drop." She hands me a harness that's connected to a jump wire. "I won't be able to jump with you because you know the bowling ball. But there's teams out there we will radio in and get someone closer before you go." We stand on the side and look for any signs of a house. All I think about images of Lucy and Lila. If anything happens to either of them I will not recover. They have became my whole world. Before them my work was my life. Now they are... I love Lila as if she's my own kid. We watch games together, I get her ready for bed. I could tell you anything in the world about her.... what's that? My eye catches something through the woods. "Lopez, over there." "Hey stop here." She tells the pilot. After 20 minutes of canvassing I see it. A small cottage. "It's the only place in these damn woods. It's got to be." She tells him. "Okay let's hover over here. You drop down a few miles away and wait for a team. Tim I'm serious wait for a team." She looks me in the eyes. "Lila is most likely in there. You don't want to risk him hurting her." "You have my word." I look at her with a serious look. I've known her since the Academy and we have became best friends. I'm her Man of Honor in her wedding a few days. I won't let her down. "All clear begin the descend." She tells the pilots. I am lowered down in the harness and look around. I don't see anyone. "Touchdown successful." I radio in. "I'll meet up with you in 3 Nyla radios in." "Copy that. I'm going to scope out the area." "10-4."

Once Nyla meets up with me I show her and Nolan the best route. They informed there's back up coming and there 10 minutes out. "Let's get a look in the window and see if we need to enter sooner. As far as we know it's just Emmett." I explain to them. "Okay, but let me look." Nyla tells me and nod. She creeps under one of the windows and peeks in. Her face softens. "Hey, Lila is in that room. Alone." She says. "Okay, what do we do?" "I say we get her out and wait for back up for Lucy. Lila is our top priority." "Yeah she is." I smile at the thought of getting her out of there. One down . One to go. "Let me see if I can open the window." She pulls out the screen quietly and looks again to make sure it's still safe. When she's it's clear she pushes it up a bit. "You should get her she knows you." Nyla nods her head in my direction. "Okay. Yeah." I push the window the rest of the way and Lila looks at me. I put my finger on my lips to show her to be quite. "Come here, baby. Tim got you." I whisper. She walks over to me and I help pull her out of the window. "Hey baby. Are you okay?" I pull her in for a hug and kiss her forehead. I inspect her for wounds. And only find a small cut on her cheek and a bruise on her head. "Yes. You save mommy?" She asks in a tiny voice. "Yeah." That's when the calvary appeared through the tree line. "Hey someone take her and head back." I wave someone over. "Here I got her. Officer Rogers." "Officer Bradford. You guard her with your life. You got me? Or you lose your badge. Better yet." I scope out another person in the line, "you, go with them. Guard her with your life as well. You got me?" "Yes sir." "Lila honey, my friends are going to watch you while I go save mommy okay? You be a good girl and I will see you soon. I love you, you are every bit my daughter as you are your mommy's you hear me?" I stop the tears from pricking in my eyes. "I love you." She hugs me and I hand her off. "Okay guys. We don't know the status of Officer Chen. But because Lila was alone we are assuming she is still alive." Harper fills the back up in. "Tim and I are going to climb in that bedroom window. And you guys are going to kick that door open." "Once we're inside we will all count to 10, you can't radio in incase Lang hears you." We go over and both climb quietly in the window. 1.2.3.4.5.6.7.8, "9,10." I say the last 2 numbers out loud and open the bedroom door at the same time I hear a loud bang from the front of the house.

Lucy's POV I wake up again, from knocked out. My hands are untied and I see Emmett standing with his back away from me looking through a bag. "Dammit, dammit, dammit," he was throwing the stuff from the bag around. I look around for a weapon and see a fire poker. I inch over quietly and grab it. Let me tell you it hurts like hell to move. My pants are discarded and I'm only in my uniform T-Shirt. I see my underwear and I quickly grab them as I push down the urge to vomit. Okay I slip one leg in and the another. And I accidentally cause something to fall over. My snap up at Emmett who turns around quicker than I've ever seen him move. "Well well, you took your good old time to kill me and look where you are now." I have the fire poker in my hand. "Your going to either A. going to let me lock you in the closet and call for help. Or B. we fight this out." I raise an eyebrow at him. He reaches in his pants but come up wide eyed and empty handed. "Oh? Looking for that." I tilt my head in the direction of his eyes and see where he left his gun. "You son of a bitch." He glares at me. And walks backwards. He is in the kitchen so I'm going to guess he's going for knife. "Well it looks like option B." I say and charged at him. I swing my weapon and miss. He reaches forward with his knife and misses me. I pull back and thrust forward with my weapon again. This time I get him in the arm and he cries out. "You ready to change your mind?" I ask. "Not a chance. Til your dead bitch." He lunges at me to attack and we both wrestle around. I felt a sharp pain in my leg and feel warm liquid run down it. I sneak out from under him bring the poker up above his head and drive back down into his chest his eyes go big and I watch him bleed out to there's nothing a breath left in him. I drop to the ground and pull my legs to my chest and cry. That's when I hear a loud bang and, "police put your hands up." I stand up quickly and put my hands in the air.   "Lucy." Tims eyes are huge as he takes in the scene before him. He runs and pulls me into his arms. "It's over." He says.   "Tim I killed him." I say. Lila! Oh my god she can't see this. "Oh my god Lila!"   "It's okay I got her out of the room before we breached the house." I sigh in relief and go back to holding on to Tim.   "I know, I know... it will be okay. Are you okay?" He asks. "Why are you..." he holds me out and sees how I'm dressed and realization hits his face, "oh my god." "Your arm, he shot you. How is it?" I change the subject quickly. "Clear through. Couples stitches and a pouty lip to Lopez and I was back on the hunt." He shrugs. "Im sorry Officer Chen, we're going to have to take your statement." Lopez comes up to me and I stare at her wide eyed. "You know the rule. It's obvious what happened here but it needs to be done." "It-it's okay I'm ready." I squeeze Tim's hand and go to follow. I relive every gruesome detail with Detective Lopez about what happened. I tell her how I woke up during it and he choked me til I passed out. And then again. I told her how I gave him the option for me to allow him the chance to be turned in. And how we fought and I thought he was going to kill me so I made the move for the kill. After talking to her she hugged and me told me It was going to be okay. "He raped me... I knew he was capable of a lot but rape." I collapse in her arms as the adrenaline rush wears off.

Tim's POV Lucy did that... she really killed him. I think back to when I found her after Caleb unconscious covered in blood and broken. But this time, this time is different. She's covered in blood, crying, and relief is on her face. I look over at her and she falls down. I run over to her. "What happened? Some one get me ambulance!" I yell. "Hey, hey, she's okay. The adrenaline rush must have worn off. None of her injuries were life threatening." Angela puts her hand on my shoulder and I look up at her. I bend over pull Lucy into my arms. "Air support lower a stretcher please." Angela radios in. "10-4." In a few minutes a stretcher is lowered down. "I'll send a harness down for you." "Actually I'll meet you there." I need to go find Lila. She's probably scared and needs a familiar face. "I called Wes, he met them at the bottom of the hill. She'll be fine. Go with Lucy." I nod and the guy tells me he'll send it down.

Soon after arriving there Lucy wakes up. "Hey honey." I'm at her side in a second. "Hi," she smiles at me weakly. "Sit." She scoots over and pats the spot next to her. "I'm so sorry I let him take you," I confess. "You didn't let him, the bastard kidnapped our daughter, shot you then took me. I'd say that's one hell of a fight." "So your not going to umm zombie out on me again?" "No I actually feel relieved..." she pauses and looks at me with a face. "We just might not umm you know for awhile." "That's fine by me." I kiss her head and pull her in for a one armed hug in the bed. "I have a visitor." Wesley announces as he walks in with Lila in his arms. "Oh, my baby." She says and reaches out to grab her and pulls her in for a hug and I wrap myself around them both. "I love you both more than you'll ever know." I whisper to them.

I'll always come for you

I t's been 6 months since I killed Emmett. I am now a official Police Officer. Tim is now a sergeant at Mid Wilshire and today, today is the day I become Mrs. Bradford. Lila was officially adopted by Tim 1 week ago and I officially become a Bradford with them today. I cant stop saying it. Tamara my "puppy" has moved in with Tim and I temporarily and will be applying for a job and her own apartment soon. But for now she's like our adopted kid. "Look at you." Angela comes in smiling at me. She holds me out at arms length and smiles at me. "It seems just like yesterday I was standing here, kidnapped by a drug lord, then standing here again. And not literally here but you know what I mean!" She joked . I laughed with her. "You and Wes are great." I smile. We also decided to make Angela and Wesley Lilas official Godparents it only seemed right and they were honored. They in return asked us to be Mila's Godparents. "You ready in here? Or do I need to drive the get away car." Jackson comes waltzing in. "Very funny.

My feet are toasty warm." I smile at them. "Mommy ready?" "Yes let's go my flower girl! Remember what to do." I smile and kiss her nose. Lopez and Wesley walked out, then Tamara and Jackson and then Lila pulled baby Mila in a red wagon decorated to say ring security. The the wedding march played and I gripped my flowers and walked down the aisle, I asked John to give me away. He was the dad in our rookie group and it just made sense since I haven't spoke to my birth parents since before Lila was born. When I stepped out to walk down the aisle I caught eyes with Tim and he smiled widely at me. I walked down the aisle as slow as I could because I was eager to be married to him. We asked Sergeant Grey to officiate our wedding. We had a very small wedding, just our bridal party, Nolan, Nyla, Grace and Sergeant Grey. That's all we needed. We begin our vows, "I'll stand by you forever, and I will always come for you, Lucy. Love brought us together, but our devotion and partnership will keep us together. You brought out a side of me I never existed a side, a soft side and relit a flame in me I never knew was out. I cannot wait to face the many adventures of life together with you." "Oh wow, how do I top that," the guests giggled as I wiped my tears, "Tim Bradford, you have always tested me and pushed my limits," the other Rookies and Tim laughed at my line, "but you've always loved me for me. You picked me up more times than I can count, and every time I came out stronger, thanks to you. I can't wait to face life with you. I love you." "I love you too." He smiled softly and leaned in to kiss my forehead like he always does. "With this ring be wed." I slid his ring on his finger. "With this ring I be wed." He my ring on my finger. "By the power invested in me by the state of California, I now pronounce you man and wife. You may now kiss the bride." Grey said. And before he could finish Tim had his arm around my waist and his lips on mine. "I love you boot." "I love you Tim." "Mommy and Daddy are married." Lila came and jumped in our arms. And we walked down the beach to where Angela had set up some tents so we could enjoy the day at the beach.

Tim and I sit on a huge white circle towel that said Mr. & Mrs. and overlook our family... they may not be family by blood, but they sure are family to us. "This is perfect." I smile. "I know Mrs. Bradford." He leans in and kisses me. "You know I knew the moment I saw you that you were going to be mine one day." He tells me. "Oh really." I raise an eye brow at him. "Yes really, I just pushed it aside because of you being my rookie ... but now look at us." He leans over and kisses my temple. "Tim, I'm pregnant." I say and he looks at me and smiles and puts a hand on my belly. "I'll protect you with my life little Bradford."

www.ingramcontent.com/pod-product-compliance
Lightning Source LLC
Chambersburg PA
CBHW070631170726
48291CB00003B/975